Carve Me A Place
Copyright © 2016
J.M. Bergman

Published by TradeSpace

ISBN-13: 978-1541312289

ISBN-10:1541312287

J. M. Bergman

For Carla

Carve Me A Place

J.M. Bergman

To: Desiree ♡

Jessica Bergman

TradeSpace

J. M. Bergman

Acknowledgments

Thank you, Katie, for inspiring me to write this novel, and for all your encouragement along the way. Kyle, thank you for supporting me and helping me pursue the dream of sharing stories. Thank you, mom, for always being a great support and motivator. Shara, thank you for all your thoughts and ideas surrounding the plot and characters. Thank you, Deborah, for your notes and great suggestions. Kara, thank you for your feedback and questions that gave me ideas for further character development. Thank you, Art Slade, for your tips and 'logical' advice!

J. M. Bergman

Prologue

11:11 PM, Saturday

They had stopped screaming.

Their expressions had been so confused when he did it. So lost. But now they lay quietly in his back seat, asleep. That's how he preferred to view it. Not drugged.

People would miss them, and he knew that wasn't fair.

But life wasn't fair. It never had been. And it was time for his life to get better.

Chapter 1

Twenty minutes earlier

"What an epic way to die!" Teagan exclaimed.

Fifteen-year-old, Annie Jeffreys elbowed her best friend in the ribs. "Violence isn't really my thing." The theatre atmosphere popped around them as they made their way to the exit and she pulled her blue sweater tighter around her olive colored skin. A man in a dark coat stepped close and collided with her petite frame.

"Hey! Watch it, you -" *Check yourself, Jeffreys; lead by example.* A life lesson from the soccer team. Other girls with dead moms could act out with destructive behaviour, but she lived differently because Coach had taught her to choose her own destiny. Survival was a choice.

"Wasn't your step-mom supposed to be here by now to pick us up?" Teagan grinned and waved at someone she knew.

"Yeah, but she's not answering her cell. What time did you tell your mom you'd be home?"

"Oh, it's fine, mom doesn't care, and dad isn't coming home tonight; some kind of overnight job or something." She shrugged.

Annie held her gaze. "You're not going to get into trouble, right?" Teagan grinned and Annie shook her head and dialed again. "Lydia?" She covered her other ear to block out the noise. Yeah, we *were* ready at 10:30. What - no, we have practice in the morning and Teagan has to get home, so we need to be picked up now. I called you as soon as the movie was done but you didn't pick up...Yes, we're outside!" She sighed and pocketed the cell.

"Bus?" Teagan leaned against the cool brick wall and slipped out her own phone.

"Sure, I'll just let the team know we'll miss practice tomorrow because some creep will follow us off the bus and kill us." Teagan burst out laughing. "Hey, shhh," Annie grimaced at the unwanted attention. A man and woman paused mid-conversation to notice them. The man had a large backpack. Annie turned away, "I wish my dad would trust us to call a cab."

Teagan gazed at the glowing clouds above the city. "He's overprotective, Ann. Your mom was in a cab when she died, right?" She stuffed her hands into her black sweater pockets. "It's nice that your dad looks out for you like that."

"I guess so." She pressed her lips together and stared blankly ahead. Green and orange lights lit a small diner across the street. A man

11

in a fedora sat alone at a table outside with a pipe hanging from his shadowed face. She couldn't tell if he was watching them, but he made her uncomfortable.

"Let's get out of here. Lydia knows one way to get here so we'll meet her on the way."

"Okay, your call." Teagan smirked and spun away from the building, half shielding her eyes from a set of headlights that pulled up to the entrance. "Come on! Turn off your brights!" A pair of nearby smokers turned their way. Her outbursts needed work. Coach would have her doing laps of the parking lot if he were here. They walked across concrete and stepped onto the sidewalk. Hopefully they'd be alone now for their short journey. Well, if Lydia didn't show up it would be a forty-minute walk. A long journey for fifteen year olds at 11:00 pm.

Light flooded around them again.

"Turn off your brights, people, we're in the middle of a city!" Teagan turned and squinted at the stopped vehicle as if the driver owed them an explanation. "Is it Lydia?"

A tall silhouette stepped in front of the glare. Lydia wasn't that tall.

***

2:10 AM

"I've got them." Crisp air blew on his sweat-beaded neck. Deep, minty smells of evergreens and sap swam around fireflies in the dark. He stared up at the stars. "No. It was easy. Yeah, they're out." He slid the phone into a pocket and rolled his shoulders.

He'd done well - no, exceptionally well. Smooth as butter.

He thought of their limp bodies, underground and away from this world's evils. He had plans for their foreseeable futures. They were his now, and he would make them lovely. His hand folded around the knife case in his bag. Time to do a little carving - just his initials for now, that's how he started last time. Nothing deeper than cutting the surface because that would be wasteful. And he didn't waste anything.

He opened the door and jogged down the stairs to his guests with his large dog close behind.

Chapter 2

3:30 PM

Cadence Rhodes knelt at the edge of the mostly green soccer field and tied her neon soccer cleats. The sun was moderately warm. She took a breath of crisp air and gazed at several other players stretching. Coach Ryan Grey was taking note of which players had arrived, but there was still no sign of her missing classmates. She sighed, pushed herself up from her knee and brushed the grass off her black soccer socks and shorts.

"Hey, Coach!" She jogged along the edge of the field to center.

He glanced up, then continued checking names on a clipboard. "What's happening, hon?" He asked in his normal, solemn tone. A blue, hooded sweatshirt and black track pants covered his lean build. He also wore his regular black cap.

"I was wondering if I could talk to the team during huddle today." She dropped her sports bag at their feet.

14

"About what?" He glanced up and down the field.

"Teagan and Annie." He stopped writing and looked at her. "Maybe after whatever you were planning to say? Everyone is so anxious." She tightened the elastic on her curly brown ponytail and gazed up expectantly.

"Do you know something?" He crossed his arms and narrowed his eyes. "It's not good to get people's hopes up if you don't."

"I know that. But I - feel something in my heart, like, that they're okay, but we need to pray for them. You know?"

Coach raised one eyebrow, still studying her. "No idea, kid." But he offered a wink and punched her arm, then looked back at his clipboard.

"Well?"

He glanced at her again, then reached for his whistle. "Okay, sure, Rhodes."

Tweet! The shrill sound turned heads and about fifteen teenage girls ran towards them. "Let's bring it in, ladies! Come on, let's go! Hustle!" Their pace quickened, and they ended in a circle around him and Cadence. She stepped back to be out of their attention. "Stay here", he said as an aside. "As I'm sure you all heard in class, Fischer and Jeffreys are still missing. The authorities are doing everything they can. It's a good idea to stop by or call to encourage their families. Worrying won't help and nationals are in three weeks! We need to stay strong and practise hard, okay ladies?"

The team murmured in agreement.

"What was that?" He barked.

"Yes, Coach!" They shouted, mirroring his intensity on their faces.

"Okay! Rhodes has something to say." He tapped the back of her shoulder.

Right. What had she planned? "Hey guys..." Her stomach churned. These were her friends but not many shared her faith. "Well, I believe in God, and, um, I believe He knows where they are."

A light chuckle was heard from someone.

"Hey! Respect, ladies!" Coach warned.

"I'm going to say a quick prayer for them." She saw Coach remove his cap and a few girls lowered their heads, but kept their curious eyes on her. She cleared her throat and began, "Dear God, I pray that You bring them home soon. And give them hope."

A couple more scoffs erupted. Warmth spread across her face.

"Thanks, Rhodes." Coach put his cap back on and seemed to study her as he spoke. "Alright! Blake and Finley, fifty push-ups for your disrespect, then join us for laps. The rest of you: two times around the field!" He blew his whistle. "Let's go!" He dropped his whistle to his sweater and pointed down the field.

Cadence started to run and felt the cool air rushing through her hair and yellow jersey. She embraced the breeze as it cooled her face.

"Good job back there." Coach jogged up beside her.

"Thanks", she said between breaths and glanced up with a smile. He met her eyes and winked.

"Have you spoken with their parents?" He took the outside corner as they went around the end of the field.

"A couple of us dropped by during spare, but they still don't know anything. Teagan's mom burst into tears as soon as she saw us." She narrowed her mouth and exhaled, keeping her breathing even so he wouldn't criticize her. "Are you going to stop by?"

"I called both of their dads."

"That's nice." A moment passed. "Why is this happening, Coach?"

"Enough talk, Rhodes - if I finish these laps first, you'll be on the side doing push-ups!" He dashed ahead and glimpsed back over his shoulder. She laughed and sprinted to match his speed.

"And if I finish first?" Her eyes glittered with the sunlight. He glanced down with a smirk and the edges of his lips curled up into one of his rare grins.

"Then I'll do push-ups."

She grinned again and pushed ahead of him.

"I don't think so." He sprinted past and yelled instructions to another player. But by the second lap he had dropped back to motivate slower runners. When Cadence neared center, she spun and backpedaled

"Hey, Coach! You ready for those push-ups?"

He jerked his head towards her with wide eyes. "No!" He broke into a sprint.

She laughed and mockingly crossed center in slow motion. He finished just after her, shaking his head, then bent at the waist and leaned on his knees breathing hard. "Okay, kid, tell you what: *after* practice I'll do as many push-ups as you want. But I gotta run the show, you know?"

"Deal." She grinned and nodded. He straightened and faked a scowl as a few players giggled. Afterwards, the entire team, drenched in sweat, stood around and counted out loud until he pushed out one-hundred-fifty. Everyone left feeling a little better about the current circumstances.

***

Annie's father slouched in his home office chair, painfully aware this was the time of day his daughter would usually wander through the front door with her best friend in tow. He pulled his hands through his salty-blonde hair for the hundredth time.

"Simon!" Lydia Jeffreys shrieked.

He startled and lunged towards her voice, crashing into the doorframe and nearly tripping over his feet in the hallway. "Is Annie home?" High ceilings, expensive plants and other articles surrounded him in the entrance. Lydia stood at the open front door with newspapers scattered at her feet. Wisps of her light brown hair blew around her perturbed face. A crisp card trembled in her hand.

"What is it?" He took the card from her.

Michelle sipped at a dreamy blood orange margarita and stretched out in the cozy housecoat she had donned. "Yes, they're gone. No, I wasn't with him when he did it." She cradled her cell phone and gazed at her French manicured nails. The hardest part, taking two spoiled girls from their wealthy parents, was over. Now the money would be delivered tonight. Game over.

Well, almost.

"Are they dead?"

"Not yet. He still thinks we'll let them live."

Silence purred through the line.

"Don't worry. We can afford to give him time to 'play'." Sip. She extended her fingers and studied a hangnail. "He'll do as I say, when the time's right." She hung up and lay back for her to allow her fresh facial mask to set in.

And if he doesn't do exactly as I say: I'll shoot all three of them.

Chapter 3

Annie woke up slowly and shivered. Everything around her was dark, as if there had been a power outage in their neighborhood. "Dad? Dad...?" Still no answer. "Hello? Is this some kind of joke?" Her skin prickled with from the cold and she turned her head back and forth, trying to break out of the darkness. She couldn't move the rest of her body. "Teagan? Hello?" She started to yank at her unmoving legs and arms again.

"Hey, stop that. You'll hurt yourself." A low, male voice made her jump.

"Who's there?" A little '*pop!*' sounded and the faint scent of sugar wafted up to meet her. Then without warning something doughy and sweet pressed right against her lips. She turned away, "Wait -"

"Hey, take it." Authoritarian, but not threatening.

"But wait, what's going on?" She strained backwards in protest. He was silent. And his silence scared her. The cool touch of a metallic object pressed on her arm. It was flat and narrow. Goosebumps began to crawl up her spine. "Please - what's going on? Please -" The object turned and felt very sharp. It was a blade. "Ah! Okay, okay..." She opened her lips and the sticky substance was pushed into her mouth. Prongs of a plastic fork were on her tongue now. She pulled back and began to chew. Brown sugar and cinnamon. The fork came several times. Then the darkness was still again.

"It's going to be okay." His voice was low, not dangerous, but not comforting either. "I've got something for you to drink." In the next second, a plastic nozzle was at her lips. "Open your mouth."

She thought back to the blade. "Can you tell me what it is? Please?"

"Water. Come on."

She opened her mouth even though she still didn't trust him. Immediately cool liquid squirted to the back of her parched throat. More poured in each time she opened her mouth. "Thanks." The room was quiet again for a moment, then a high-pitched ripping sound made her jump. A second later a sticky covering pressed down over her mouth. She tried to turn away, but he held her head in place. "Hey, please - Mmmmm! Mmmm!!!" In the next moment, she felt his hands at the back of her head untying whatever was over her eyes. When he lifted it away, she saw a dim light hanging in front of her. As her eyes adjusted to the dark room she noticed him sit back down across from her beside a small table. She blinked several times because she didn't believe what she was seeing. But when the scene didn't change, confusion added to the fear in her eyes.

He grinned and leaned forward.

***

"Shake it off." He intertwined and steepled his fingers, covering his lips. "Look, you know me pretty well, so this doesn't need to be scary, alright? There are going to be rules - you follow my rules - and everyone stays happy. Sound fair?" He sipped at his water bottle and studied her scared eyes.

She nodded once.

"I'm an artist, did you know that? I have something nice planned for today." He watched her face a moment longer then reached for the blade. She tried to scream but her voice was suffocated by the duct tape. "No, Annie, panic isn't going to get you anywhere down here. Besides it'll look good when it's done, I promise, and you'll hardly feel a thing." He slid forward and reached for her arm.

She followed the knife with her eyes and made a surprised noise when she saw the bandaging near her wrist where his initials were. "Relax." He shook her arm lightly until it became less rigid. He began with one small cut and she immediately tensed and 'screamed' again. But the cuts were shallow and quick, and the next few got smaller responses. "You're okay." He promised.

He glanced up from his work a moment later and noticed her eyelids start to flutter and fall. He went back to work, satisfied that the drug in her water was working. He moved the knife carefully through her skin. He wasn't doing this to see her suffer, after all. That would make him a monster.

"Mm….mm" She hung her head now and her voice was so soft. Just like Teagan's had been.

"Shhhhh", he whispered. "You'll be asleep soon." His dog started barking from the other room, and he lifted a cloth and wiped the blood off his blade.

***

Simon Jeffreys clutched his hands in front of him on his leather settee. The media had drilled him all evening with the same question: Why had he and the Fischers not met the ransom terms? Well, if it had been up to him he would have given the kidnapper anything he or she wanted, and Annie would be home by now. But the lead investigator insisted that giving a partial amount would set up ongoing communication with the authorities which was a better option. So that's what they'd done, but now his mind swam with destructive possibilities of what could be happening to his daughter because the half-ransom hadn't been touched and the police hadn't been contacted. The fireplace crackled across the room as a log fell to the ashes.

"Hey, you." It was the anchoring voice of his wife. He glanced up and saw her approaching, freshly showered, with a steaming cup. She kissed his forehead, and handed him the mug. "My brother called and wants you to know he's thinking of us. How are you doing?" She lowered to sit beside him.

"What do you think?" His voice was low and weak. If only he had a coin for every time he'd been asked that in the last forty-eight hours

"I think -" She rubbed the back of his neck. "That you're a good father who's doing everything you can to bring his daughter home."

"There must be something else I can do though instead of just sitting here..."

She brushed his collar. "I think you need to give yourself a break." She leaned in and kissed him, with the tropical scents of her shampoo engulfing him. She massaged his back, but he ignored her and focused on the crystal coffee table in front of them. He could have done more that night. *Should* have.

Like been a good father and left work early to pick her up like she had asked. But since his first wife passed away, he'd ignored the pain by devoting all his time to working at the hospital. And now Annie was gone too.

"Simon, are you listening to me? You've sacrificed considerably for our family with long hours at the hospital and you make the world better every time you go to work." She pinched his shoulders between her fingers and massaged with her thumbs.

He sighed and looked up at her. "Well, I needed to hear that. I just can't make sense of everything that's happened.

"Come get some rest, it'll help."

"No, I can't sleep." He met her eyes, but quickly looked down before she could lure him away. "It doesn't seem right to sleep in my warm bed when she's out there somewhere." He closed his eyes and removed his glasses. "I want to go for a drive, you know that helps clear my thoughts." He nodded swiftly as a sign that the conversation had ended, then kissed her lightly and stood. "You don't need to wait up." He started down the hallway.

"Simon… let me help you. Just tell me what I need to do."

He looked back and saw her standing with her wet hair draped over her shoulders. The lines under her eyes showed the same exhaustion he felt. This situation was hard on her too, and he needed to remember that. But he needed space so he could be strong again. For both of them. He walked back and pulled her in gently for a kiss on the forehead. "Please understand that this isn't for me to be away from you. It's for me to find my strength." He kissed her on the forehead again, and pulled away.

***

10:30 pm

"The cops must think this is some kind of joke! If they want to mess around with our demands, then I say we start cutting up those brat's bodies and show everyone who's in charge here!" She slammed the table and coffee splashed over the side of her cup.

"That wasn't part of the plan. You said as long as I made them disappear everything else would work out. Getting the money is your job." He watched the coffee turn into a stain on his wooden table.

"Well, we're on a timeline, so now the plan has changed." She glared up at him with glassy eyes.

He licked his lips and lowered onto a chair across from her. "No." Adding the intricate designs to their bodies was a form of art - cutting them into pieces was criminal. He hadn't even done that to his first hostages. The girls belonged to him now and he would be the one making the calls on what happened to them. He'd even chosen the underground bunker outside of the city because he knew they'd be hidden and safe there.

"Do you think this is a game?" She pushed her chair back and stood. "All or nothing, right? You can't just back out because it's getting hard!"

"Hey!" He stood and towered over her. "I took them without a trace, because when I do something, I do it right the first time. They're fascinating humans, not dolls we can cut up." His other three victims hadn't been fascinating until they met his knife. No, their hearts were layered with abuse, alcohol, and murder. Dark and dirty. But these girls were different. And he would never destroy them.

"You're a coward."

He grabbed her shoulders and saw some intensity drain from her face. He waited a moment and took a breath to let his anger pass, because he'd never resort to violence against a woman. "Look, today was rough. Why don't we grab some wine, relax, and talk this over in an hour or so?" She was toxic, yet stunning, and perhaps part of what drew him to her was the destruction hidden beneath her makeup. She pulled him into a hard kiss and a piece of his heart numbed with pleasure.

"I'm not doing anything until all the money comes in." She stated and slipped away. By the time he blinked free of her spell, she was grabbing her coat off the back of a wooden chair.

He slid his hands into his pockets. "I'm not hurting them like that. Find another way."

She spun back with her eyes blazing. He didn't let it show, but he felt unnerved. "Figure something else out then, or I'm taking over and putting an end to this." She was moving back towards him, fast, and he almost started to wonder why his life wasn't flashing before his eyes. If she didn't calm down she'd probably injure him or have an

29

aneurysm in his house - not something he wanted to explain to anybody.

"Okay, calm down. Grab me a phone charger, I have an idea."

J. M. Bergman

Chapter 4

6:00 AM

Teagan's mind blurred as she slowly woke up. The light beneath the door cast shadows into the empty, concrete room where they sat on a sleeping bag. Her nose tickled with the cold even though a thin blanket had been draped around her. She wanted a hot shower in the bathroom where she could be surrounded by light and privacy. Annie leaned against Teagan's bare, bandaged arm. Having her best friend here was a source of comfort, but also a tear in her heart, because there was no way she could help her through this pain when she was just as much a prisoner herself.

Footsteps approached.

No... Please ... let it be someone here to rescue us. A similar plea to what her mind begged from the darkness of her childhood bedroom where she and her mom would often hide. The door opened, flooding unnatural light into their cell. She squinted and ducked her head sideways. It was him. Anger and fear swelled in her chest, and her breathing quickened.

Get away from us, you monster!

That's what she wanted to scream. But duct tape still covered her mouth. A tear slipped down her cheek.

"Hey, sweethearts. You awake?" He called in a low voice. Neither could answer because of the tape over their mouths. Annie moaned and began to move beside her. A bright light flashed from his hand and when her vision cleared she saw him looking down at a phone. He stuffed it into his back pocket, then walked forward until he stood in front of them. He lowered to his haunches and draped an arm over his knee. "How'd you two sleep? Either of you need to use the bathroom?" He smelt of coffee and spicy aftershave. Scents that carried memories of listening to his advice, following his actions, and looking up to him for leadership. Those were some of her favorite reflections over the last two years. She nodded and didn't try to hide the anger in her glare. "Yeah?" His face was covered with shadows. "Alright." He grabbed her feet and easily pulled her forward. "I'll cut you loose. You've got ten minutes." He reached into his bag and produced the knife. *No!* Memories of the cuts to her arms flashed across her mind. She squirmed and managed to pry her Converse shoes from his grip. "Hey! Stop that. I'm just here to let you use the washroom and have a snack if you want. Alright?"

Did she have a choice? Yes, she had choices, but she knew from experience that not doing what she was told came with painful

33

consequences. She stopped moving and he grabbed her feet again and began to cut the duct-tape around her ankles.

"Use the bathroom and leave the open the door when you're done. I want to come in and look at your bandages and maybe clean them up today." She turned her torso, as she'd grown accustomed to doing when he would reach behind to cut the tape from her sore wrists. He cut carefully and a moment later her hands dropped free. He ripped the tape off. "Go." He turned to Annie who had been watching them quietly. "What about you?"

Teagan rolled over onto her knees. Bracing on the wall with one hand, she slowly rose to shaky legs. *Take one step at a time.* Her feet were heavy. Now another step. And another. She realized she was standing behind him now. Between him and the open door.

How far could it be to a door or window?

She glanced back and saw that he was still distracted. She faced the lit doorframe again and took a breath. *Bolt!* She sprinted through the door into the unnatural light. A steel staircase loomed in the middle and a dark tunnel to the side. No windows. And then his arm was around her waist and dragging her backwards. She kicked back hard.

He didn't even flinch.

She screamed and thrashed her arms and legs as he pulled her back into the room of shadows. This was it, she had messed up.

***

Simon rubbed his temples. Fatigue was setting in bringing migraines, insomnia and all the side effects that came as a result. He reached for the bottle of Advil he'd been keeping on his desk and tossed two back without water. Years prior to this, and even prior to losing his beautiful wife, Maria, had been used meticulously to build his career, buy his mansion, and create a family. He now saw that focusing on the first of these goals had essentially cost him the last, and most important. He closed his eyes and could see Maria laughing and singing with her Spanish accent, her beautiful brown eyes sparkling above that perfectly shaped smile. Her blue summer dress blowing in the breeze as she walked along a rocky brook.

He shook his head and pulled his hands through his hair. His gaze landed on the black leather Bible he had found in a box of Maria's treasured items. He'd cracked it open last night to her favorite section: Psalms. The words had been poetic, likely written by someone undergoing deep turmoil. The text revealed that the author, for whatever reason, believed his cries for help were being heard by his god. Simon personally believed in no such thing as a higher power, but he had empathized with the author. The words had lifted his own soul. He noticed that the text was numbered, similar to Shakespeare. The number, ninety-one, was written in large bold letters.

Ninety-one? His hand ran over his brow. *How many of these are there?* He sighed and looked at the clock. He needed sleep, but he also needed a distraction from the terrible thoughts tormenting him. So he began to read:

"Those who live in the shelter of the Most High
Will find rest in the shadow of the Almighty."

He read it again. The '*Most High*'; the '*Almighty*. Those were likely terms that religious people used to talk about their god. Well, it sounded alright. A nice thing to believe if it were true. He read on. A few sentences later he came across a line that would stay in his mind for the rest of the day.

"The Lord says, I will rescue those who love me."

***

Teagan could barely breathe as her back was slammed against a cold wall and Coach pinned her in place. All she could hear was his breath pushing through his teeth above her.

"What were you thinking?" He finally spat. His words hung for a moment. Then he slapped the wall beside her face. "Damnit, Teagan!" She whimpered and flicked her head in the opposite direction. She tried to plead through the duct tape but he slapped the wall again and she shut her mouth. "Do you remember what I told you?"

She nodded fast. Cold sweat caked her forehead and tears formed in her eyes. She'd been brave a moment ago, but now he stood above her as a hurricane of strength. Her fear grew and she began to cry. He growled and looked at the floor for a moment, then ripped the duct tape away.

"Ah!" Her face stung and tears streamed down her cheeks. She shivered with cold and fear, and felt her strength leave. If it wasn't for his hand still holding one arm against the wall she was sure she'd collapse. He grabbed a bandaged section of her arm and she cried out again.

"What was that?" He yelled.

"I - I -"

"You're drugged and weak, in *my* territory, which means you follow my rules. I told you not to try anything, didn't I? Didn't I?"

"Yes!" She tried to pull away and her head came up against the wall.

"Look - you don't have to be afraid of anything except me down here. Or was that not clear?"

She choked on her tears, but didn't dare speak.

He dropped his head with a slow exhale. "I don't want to hurt you, Teagan." When he'd yell at her on the field and drop his head like that, it usually meant the confrontation had ended and his lecture was over. Maybe this was it; another warning. A shudder passed through her body again, and she began to shake uncontrollably. Shock and relief. "Did you think you could outrun me? Honestly?"

This wasn't over. She licked her lips and tried to take a full breath.

"Come on, you're smarter than that! What was your plan after getting through that door?"

"I don't -" She whispered, trying to find focus by looking at the dark ground. A new knot began building in her stomach.

"What?" He demanded, louder than before.

She jerked her head back up. "I don't know…" Her shoulders shook with her sobs now. "Why are you doing this? I -I mean, I'm - I'm sorry about -"

"Hey, what have I told you about tears? They get you nowhere, on or off the field." He paused. "Try again."

She took a quick breath, "I - I shouldn't have run." She curled her fingers into the balls of her hands. "I'm sorry." Her whispered words hung in the otherwise silent space. She could feel his hot breath on her face, just inches away.

"You're right." His voice was still weighty, but his grip relaxed. "Thank you for the apology."

She bit her tongue, unsure if he'd let her speak. "Why are you doing this, Coach?"

A moment passed before he answered. "The world is bigger than just you and I, hon." He released her arms and she fell forward. He caught her shoulder and eased her back against the wall. The concrete cooled the heat that had spread up her back. Her knees felt as if they would snap under her weight. "Fifty push-ups."

"What?" She looked up at his shadowed face.

"Drop. Now."

She blinked and tried to form words. Her legs wobbled beneath her. The darkness that covered the floor made her shiver again. "I - I don't think I can..."

"Try. I have time."

"But, I -"

"Drop. You of all people know you can't step out of line and get away with it. Not with me." His tone hardened.

"Okay…" She slid out from under his hand, down the wall until she sat on her knees. Then placed her hands on the cold, dark floor. The coolness spread up her arms. "Can I try from my knees?"

His silhouette lowered to a crouch beside her. "That's fine." He placed his hand on her head and eased her down into position. "Bring your head up to touch my hand every time."

"Okay", she breathed. She focused her weight and very slowly went down a few inches and pushed back up. "Uhh…I can't…"

"One." He eased her down again. *Down, up.* Her form was awful, but he wasn't commenting on it. "Two. Three."

Breath in, breath out. Her cheeks burned, but the cold spread up through her knees now.

"Five. Six."

Keep going. Keep pushing.

"Seven."

She pulled up and paused. Her body ached from the cold and her movements.

"Come on. Keep going." He didn't sound angry.

"I... don't think...I can...make..."

"You got yourself into this. You should have planned for consequences." He pushed her down again.

"Wait -" Her body shook between hot and cold flashes. It was hard to breathe. "Please, I -"

"Give me five more."

"I'll try." She whispered. *Push, Teagan.* Her elbows shook and she was soaked in sweat. Her body dipped a couple inches and came back up.

"Good. Again."

She bent at the elbows again and shook violently. Then cement crashed against her face. The fall should have hurt, but she felt nothing.

"Okay, that's enough for now." He pulled her up by a shoulder but she fell lopsided against his raised knee. "Teagan... Hey, get up." She tried to right her body but couldn't move. Black and light flashed in front of her and her insides were burning. "Teagan?" He pressed his cool hand against her burning forehead, then grabbed her arms to look at her face dead on. "Hey!" He snapped his finger in front of her. "Come on, stay with me."

Darkness was overtaking her vision. "I need...throw up..." She managed to wheeze, just before everything turned black and heat exploded inside her body. The cool concrete beneath her vanished and air rushed over her face. But heat continued to spread down her body. Icy, cold particles hit her. She gasped and her eyes flew open. Bright light crashed around her. Then cold again. Hot. Cold. And again. She heard the sound of running water.

Splash!

"- you hear me? Teagan?" More water splashed up at her. She blinked down at the white sink in front of her. His hand was beneath the water, spraying it back up to her face. His other arm held her up. The water came again. She coughed and grabbed the sink with both hands. Her vision blurred with the next spray of water. Her body began to cool and she lifted some of her own weight. Then her stomach convulsed. She pushed away and fell to her knees in front of the toilet. Contents pushed up her throat and spewed out her mouth without permission. She coughed and held her chest while tears fell from her clenched eyes. A hot wave pushed through her body again. She stayed on the floor until only strings of spit fell from her mouth. Finally, she sat back on her knees and wiped saliva away with the back of her arm. She could feel the blood pumping through her veins again and strength crept back. She looked around; he was gone. She pushed up and closed the door. Then washed her hands and face and used the toilet. A shower would be so nice right now. A knock sounded at the door and when she opened it, he placed a water bottle in her hand.

"You okay?"

She nodded and drank, still feeling his gaze on her.

"Take a seat. I want to clean up your bandages." He closed the toilet lid and she sat down.

"Can I have a shower?"

He started to unwrap her bandages and considered her request. "No."

Her shoulders fell. "But I'm covered in sweat and I smell like vomit."

He set his supplies on the sink. "Well, now you'll remember what happens when you step out of line." He tipped the bottle of peroxide onto a cloth.

I hate you so much! I wish you were dead! But even as she let her anger build she knew those thoughts wouldn't help the situation. *Focus on the good things.* "Thanks for the water." She inhaled it while he unwrapped her other arm.

"Yeah, kid." The peroxide burned and she grit her teeth through the pain. He wrapped on fresh, dry bandages a few seconds later. She noticed his muscles moving beneath his dark, cotton sleeved shirt. His physique had motivated her to train hard and he'd been her role model. Strong and unwavering. She hated herself for ever having those thoughts. "Okay, you're good to go."

She met his eyes with a look of defiance. The new bandaging helped her feel better but she refused to thank him for it. None of this should be happening. She followed him back to the wall where Annie sat whimpering. *Annie!* She'd been so lost in what was happening that she'd forgotten about her friend.

"Annie, I'm okay. Don't worry about it." The sound of fresh duct tape being unrolled distracted her. She watched him do his dirty work as he began to bind her ankles together again. "I looked up to you!"

"Well, hon, I guess you've learned a hard life lesson", he dropped her legs to the floor. "Not everyone is who they seem to be." Annie shook with sobs beside them. "Stop that."

Teagan looked back at her friend and was about to speak when she saw the fresh duct tape coming down over her face. "No! Please -" She whipped her face to the side and her brown hair fell across her face and eyes.

He straightened her chin. "Come on, no more trouble today, alright?"

"I can't help it! It's hard to breathe with it on my mouth."

Annie sobbed beside her.

"Ugh…" He grunted and glanced Annie's way. He brought the roll of tape back to his mouth with one hand and ripped off a piece. Teagan twisted her face away again. He waited until she glanced back. "This is happening, Fischer. Come on." She glared up at him but held her tongue. The tape came down over her mouth. Annie was hyperventilating now. "Ann-ie", he sighed in a low voice. He sat back on his haunches again and ripped the duct tape off her face so she could breathe. She began to gasp for air and choke on the mixture of oxygen and tears.

"Aah!" She eventually screamed up at him.

Teagan's stomach churned with emotion and the fear of what he might do to Annie.

"What was that?" He retorted. Annie flinched and tried to regain composure. Her shoulders rose and fell with each shallow breath. Ryan shook his head. "You know, if you ladies keep doing this you'll suffocate. Then nobody gets to be happy."

Annie slowly lifted her head. "Coach!" She screamed through her tears. From the light shining into the room they could see the edge of his lips curl upwards.

J. M. Bergman

Chapter 5

"Breathe." Ryan Grey continued to watch Annie gasp for air. Hearing her say his name with emotion and disgust intrigued him. "There, that's better. Come on, one more breath. Good." He snatched the roll of tape off the concrete and ripped off a piece with his teeth. "Alright, hold still."

"No!" She screamed, whipping her hair sideways. "Please, Coach! You don't have to do this!" He frowned into the darkness but didn't retaliate. He wouldn't react to outbursts of emotion like that, and she, unlike Teagan, knew better than to push him.

"Are you finished?" He caught the angry, yet fearful disbelief in her eyes. Her breathing was still shallow. "Annie, breathe from your stomach, not your chest. You know that." She closed her lips and he noted her shoulders stopped moving. "Good." He lifted the tape to her mouth. "And it's, 'Ryan'. I'm not your coach anymore."

"Wait -"

"Oh, so you're running things in here now?" Establishing authority was important, but he could afford some lenience with this one. Besides, her naive thoughts made things interesting.

"I don't..." She stopped and her lips twisted into a pout. "This isn't you, *Ryan*." She said his name as if it were a word from a foreign language and her voice cracked. Some mascara she had missed when cleaning off in the shower left a smudge under her eye.

"I'll be the judge of who I am." He flattened the tape against her skin. "And you need to get a hold on your emotions because none of this is going away." She wasn't fighting him now and that was good. He leaned in with his thumb to wipe the makeup away, and she closed her eyes to let him. But then narrowed her brows in a sulk, without thanking him when he finished. He decided to let the moment pass as propped himself on one knee again so he could see them both at the same time.

"See? You ladies are stronger than you give yourselves credit for." He said it to keep their spirits brave. Helpless victims were boring. Like his parents who gave up after only a few days. He stood and stepped back.

Why did Teagan have to make things difficult today?

She'd always had too much spunk for her own good. He honestly didn't want to lay a hand on her, but he almost had. Almost lost control. And that was something he'd sworn would never happen again. But a crazy stunt like this couldn't happen again either. Annie was crying again and Teagan turned and nudged her with sad eyes.

47

There we go.

"So, Teagan broke the rules today." She whipped her head back to him, with fear written on her features. He lowered back in front of her. "This is so we're clear that today is the last time. And remember: you asked for it." Her eyes grew wide and he moved quickly. She flinched, but he snatched Annie up by the waist instead and slung her over his shoulder. Annie began to scream and kick as he carried her out the door and looked back. "Break the rules and Annie gets a drug-free session with me."

"Mmmm! Mmmm!" Teagan screamed. She kicked up and down on the concrete wildly like a child and she managed to roll up on her knees and inch forward.

He glared down at her. "Stay there. Don't make this worse."

Tears streaked her face. "Mmm!" She snuck a bit further, but she lost her balance and fell to the floor. Ryan left the door open and stepped out.

"Don't worry", he muttered to Annie. "I'll put you out after I'm done."

"Mmm! Mmm!" She screamed and kicked his stomach. Dramatic youth. He wouldn't do much, but he'd let her feel it. He had to. If he knew these two well, this would be the game ender for Teagan.

"Stop. You'll get over it eventually, and you might not even remember." He unlocked the door. He'd use the same drug from the first night when he'd followed them from the theatre and offered them a ride. He'd reprimanded them for walking alone that late at night,

48

threatened to bench them at the next game and took their phones right away. He said it would help them to remember not to walk home alone at that hour and that he'd give them back when he dropped them off. Then he'd mentioned something about needing gas and drove them away from their rich neighborhood for the last time. After they were in a quiet alley it had been easy to cover both their faces with a towel drenched in chloroform.

Annie landed a hard kick under his ribs and cleared his memories. He flinched but didn't let her see it.

"You're gonna pay for that one." He threw her onto the chair and whipped the knife out of his pocket. The room felt darker than usual.

***

The next morning

"Local News Broadcaster, Kari Steele, coming to you from the Police Station, where the cell phone of kidnapped victim, Anna-Marie Jeffreys, was recovered this morning from an FBI window-sill overlooking the sidewalk and -"

Simon shut it off and set the Bible down beside him. Yes, the police had recovered Annie's phone this morning, with a picture of the girls, and one message in the inbox. The message stated that unless the full ransom was delivered at eleven o'clock, Saturday morning, one of the girls would be killed. The photo was unsettling: the girls had their mouths covered and their hands behind their backs. They were both in tank tops and jeans, with what looked like bandaging wrapped around sections of their arms. The officers had let them see the picture and date-stamp on the phone before insisting they needed to scour it for evidence.

"I don't know what to say." Lydia placed the remote in her lap. Sunlight gleamed off her silver bracelets and rings. The coffee machine gurgled from the kitchen and the beautiful aroma of a fresh brew filled the air. "We'll get through this, Simon." She grabbed his hand. "One incident at time."

"Hmm", he grunted and absently pulled skin on the side of his face. The ceiling fan turned above them and provided some cool air to think.

"Isn't it strange that the drop location is so public?" A tropical aquarium gurgled next to the settee.

"The main train transit station? No, that's common, I believe. This way the criminals can blend back into the crowd." He wiped his hand across his forehead. "That's what they hope to do, I'm sure."

"Well I guess that makes sense." She massaged the back of his neck with artistry.

"The officer I spoke with said we can't be there, but I have something else to say about that." He reached forward and took a mint from the glass bowl on the coffee table. He tossed it in his mouth and instantly began to chew. "I'll be there. I want to see these dirt bags for myself."

"Don't you dare say that!" She grabbed his arm. "The message on Annie's phone said if it even *'appears'* that anyone is following after the pickup, one of them will be shot! You can't take that chance, Simon! Or what if a gun is pulled on you? You're a doctor - this isn't your playing field." Her grip relaxed as her words sunk in. "Let's let the authorities do this and bring our daughter home." She rested her chin on his firm shoulder.

Simon looked straight ahead. He slowly let out a breath and brought his hands together. "Yeah. Yeah, you're right." He sighed.

The Lord says, I will rescue those who love me.

He ignored his wife's presence and focused on the words instead. A verse his dear Maria would have loved. One she'd probably put to a Mexican tune at their piano. But he'd told her early on that he didn't believe in those things, so she'd stopped sharing her poetic gifts with him. But now with nothing left to turn to, he desperately wanted those words to be true.

***

Light fell across Annie's face and her heavy eyelids opened. She'd been dreaming about a man dressed in white reaching a hand down to her. He had been smiling with warm eyes. But now everything around her was covered in shadows. Was this another dream? A tall figure stood in the light of the doorframe. It suddenly moved closer and she screamed, but her voice was muffled.

"Morning." The dark silhouette offered. He stooped down in front of her. The voice was familiar and made her stomach churn. He reached for her face and in a quick motion, tape ripped across her mouth.

"Oww!" She cried out and tried to bring her hand to her face to push the pain back, but her hands were stuck behind her back. Her muscles and joints cringed too. Through watery eyes she could see this man watching her. He wore a sports jacket, track pants and a cap.

"Coach?" She blinked. *Where were they, and why would he be here waking her up?*

"Too early, maybe?" He mused.

Her eyes began to adjust to her surroundings. The cold floor, dark walls around her, a head on her shoulder. "Why -"

"Shake it off." He squirted cold water at her face from the bottle in his hand.

"Wait!" She shook her head and coughed, then took several breaths from her stomach - *why did that feel important?* - and the dark details began to flash back. The cutting room, drugs, duct tape... "No!" She shook her head and she drilled his eyes with the same expression

52

as when she realized who her captor was. "No! Ryan, no!" Her forehead rippled with disbelief and disappointment.

"There we go." He smirked. Teagan stirred beside her. "Oh, you're both awake." *Rip*! He tore the tape from her face and squirted her in the face too. Teagan hacked and gasped for air.

"Ahhh! Hey!" She screamed, sputtering and tossing her head. "Ugh, why'd you have to do that?" He squirted her again and she screamed and shook her head. "I hate you!" She coughed and stumbled over a run of complaints. He watched and waited. Then squirted her again and she responded the same way.

"I'll stop whenever you do." She scowled but grew quiet. After a moment, he spoke. "No trouble today, got it?"

She continued coughing and finally spat to the side. "Okay, whatever."

"What was that?" His authority didn't carry anger but it demanded respect. She cleared her throat then stared at him silently. He held her gaze and waited. "No trouble."

"Yeah. I got it." He watched her silently, as if deciding whether or not he was satisfied. She stared back in defiance. "When do we get to see these cuts for ourselves?"

"You see them every time I clean your bandages."

"Are you kidding? You expect me to look while you're burning my skin away with peroxide?"

"That lip of yours needs an adjustment."

"Yeah, well -" She started to cough again.

"Teagan, are you okay?" Annie glanced between her and Ryan. Watching them fight yesterday had been terrifying. She'd been so scared he'd kill her. Teagan faced her and gasped.

"Annie!" Then wide-eyed back to Ryan. *Cough.* "You're letting us talk to each other?"

"I find your jabber amusing. When you're polite", he added. This was the first time since arriving that sentences had been exchanged between the three of them. How strange, to finally have a real conversation. Spicy cologne scents floated around him and with it came memories of team huddles and standing beside him before being sent onto the field. Back when she'd hung on every word he said. That seemed like another lifetime now.

"Aren't you worried we'll scream for someone to help us?" Teagan ventured, yanking Annie's mind back to the present; to the cold, dark place where she was a hostage at the hands of the man whom she would have trusted with anything.

He crossed one arm over his knee. "No, you're smarter than that. What would your plan be if nobody heard you, huh? Because I'm still right here, and we can repeat yesterday if that's what you want." He paused. Then, "Actually, go ahead, scream for help and see what happens. Keep in mind, I let you listen to Annie scream last night." The rest of yesterday's details came back to Annie, and she drew in a thin breath. It had all happened so quickly. Right when it seemed that he'd moved on from Teagan's reckless actions, he seemed to snap. He'd grabbed her, the innocent one, and taken his anger out on her. Without

54

warning the knife cut into her arm as he held her in place from behind and dragged long lines through her skin. The pain was excruciating. Somehow, she'd made it back to this room, though she couldn't remember how. She loved Teagan dearly, but that wasn't the first time they'd gotten into trouble because of her brash decisions.

Neither of them made a sound.

"See? I knew you ladies were smart. And before you get yourselves into trouble again, I want you to know we're underground. Miles from the city."

Underground?

That sunk in for a silent moment, like an anchor, and pulled and hope of escaping down with it. He looked at both their faces individually.

"But if no one can hear us, why have you had our mouths taped shut?" Annie asked softly, carefully.

"A couple of reasons", he began as he shrugged off his backpack. He pulled out his knife and spun it once with ease. "Number one: mind games, really." He looked her in the eyes and lightly punched her leg, then started cutting the tape around her ankles. "Number two: If I let you girls talk to each other when I'm not here, who knows what kind of mischief you'd get into." He ripped the tape off her jeans.

Teagan scoffed and asked, "What do you mean by 'underground'? Are we in some weird kind of basement?"

He propped himself on one knee. "Ever heard of a bunker? Military had them all over the place for different reasons. Jada and I found this one during an afternoon run." Pride etched his voice.

"Yeah, but where are we? Didn't anyone notice you bring us here?" Teagan pushed, as if he owed them an answer.

Ryan cleared his throat. "We're in a forest, kid. And if you want me to let you talk, you better watch your tone."

She pressed her lips together. "Sorry."

He cleared his throat again and opened his mouth to demand a louder answer. Both girls saw it and knew the expression.

"I mean, *sorry*", she enunciated. He narrowed his eyes at her.

"Ryan, how did you get us out here?" Annie interjected before another fight started. "If we're in a forest, away from the road, did you carry us? Wasn't it hard?"

"Are you kidding? My bag weighs more than the two of you." He rose. "Come on, get up. You can walk today." He helped her to her feet by lifting near her shoulder. Her head reached just below his chest. "You need the bathroom?"

"In a bit." She was surprised that he would allow some freedom. Especially after Teagan's escape attempt. Perhaps he trusted her more.

"Your new bandages look like they're holding up alright. They feel okay?" She hadn't even noticed them. Which probably meant she'd passed out from the pain while he cut her yesterday.

"Oh. I guess so." She looked down at her arms. "When did -"

"Ryan?" Teagan called from the floor. He glanced down at her.

"Can I keep the tape off my mouth while you're with Annie? It's easier to breathe. And you just said it doesn't matter if I scream." She waited and bit her lip in the silence. Annie closed her eyes and frowned. If a word-filter product was ever invented she'd buy one for Teagan. Or maybe she could kindly suggest to Ryan later that he not let give Teagan the freedom to talk. Ryan stooped to Teagan's eye level and studied her incredulously.

"After yesterday - you're asking me for a favor?" His tone was quiet and frightening. Teagan drew her head back and pressed against the wall. "You broke my trust and lost my respect. And now you'll need to earn that back, kid." He picked up the roll of tape. "Until then, no favors." It came down on her mouth. Then he stood and nudged Annie out of the room.

This was the first time she'd been standing outside of their cell, and she looked around. She noticed that he wasn't holding her bound hands. Then she saw Ryan's dog, Jada, lying to one side of the staircase about fifteen feet away watching them.

"Don't talk to her." Jada flipped her tail up and down, but she kept her head on the floor. The sound of a loud generator came from somewhere. The air was cool and overhead lighting shone above. A staircase led up to a door in the ceiling and there were a couple other doors, and a tunnel that led into darkness. "Don't get any ideas out here or this will be the last time I let you out on your feet." She glanced up and saw him watching her gaze. A few dark lines creased his face beneath his eyes. "I'm letting you stretch. Don't make me regret it."

57

She wouldn't run, that would be a futile decision. She could never beat him up those stairs, nor was she brave enough to venture into that tunnel. But after yesterday, it was clear that one of them had to get away somehow and find help. Ryan was dangerous.

Had he taken any other girls from the team? She needed a way to injure him and get away to warn the others before they became his next victims. Maybe there was a loose rock or a tool on the floor that she could hit him in the head with. Or if she could somehow get his knife away...but could she bring herself to stab him? She sat down and he closed the door and stepped towards her.

"Can I have my hands untied for a few minutes? My wrists are really sore."

He looked down in the dim light with hard eyes. They'd been hard on the field too, but this was a darker kind of hard, a steely anger. "Fine, just a couple minutes though." He finally said. "That's for you." A wrapped sandwich and water bottle sat on the table beside them. He stepped behind her, and cut the binds in half.

"Thank you", she whispered and brought her hands in front of her, pulling them free of the tape. She moved her fingers back and forth in front of her and saw Ryan walk to his chair, and take out his cell phone. He watched her for a moment, sat, and then gazed down at the screen in his hand. Okay, think fast. She continued to flex her fingers but scanned the room for a weapon. Nothing. The floor was clean. Well, her body could be a weapon. She had a great kicking foot and self-defence class had taught her how to knife-hand an attacker's neck. If

58

she moved quickly she could strike his neck before her foot took his groin. She narrowed her vision to the general area of her target and wiped her palms on her jeans. Her feet planted on the floor and she mapped out her moves.

Okay, lunge, punch, kick. On three: one - two -

"Hey!" She flashed her eyes up to his face. He'd been watching her.

***

Justin Reynolds parked his silver Cavalier near the curb and pushed his sunglasses onto his forehead. He was one of the counsellors at Rendel High School. He knew Annie had lost her mother at a young age and now that she had disappeared, he knew her father would likely be in a bad place emotionally.

He made his way up the granite rock work and blew out a low whistle as he took in the outstanding mansion. Massive French windows surrounded by intricate brick work, and beautiful landscaping leading up to the home.

I wasn't sure about coming here to begin with, but how am I supposed to work with this? He looked around again doubtfully as he approached the entrance. *What can I give that he doesn't already have?*

He pressed the doorbell. A gust of wind fingered through his blonde, shaggy hair. Moments later, a disheveled-looking man, whom he presumed to be Annie's father (so this is what doctors look like at home), opened the door.

"Hi there, I'm Justin Reynolds", he smiled and extended his hand, "Dr. Simon Jeffreys, is it?"

"Just Simon." The man shook his hand once and cleared his throat. "Come in, please." He pushed the door wider and motioned with his other hand.

"Thank you." Justin walked in and was taken aback by the inside of this home. Crystal light fixtures, a massive exquisite - obviously imported - rug, and tropical greens he had never seen before growing out of a tall porcelain vase met his gaze. "Nice plant." He smiled and nodded towards it, hoping to have somewhere to form a conversation. Unfortunately, Simon's expression was blank. In fact, when he glanced at the vase it was as if he were noticing it for the first time. Luckily this awkward exchange was interrupted when a striking woman emerged from another room.

"Oh, this is Lydia, my wife." Simon turned and gestured towards her.

"Hi, there", she smiled brightly and walked forward in a simple, yet sharp navy blue dress, extending her hand, "So nice of you to come." Her crisp poise made Justin feel as though he'd arrived at an interview for something in which he was extremely under-qualified. They shook hands and she stepped back towards her husband.

"Thank you for having me." He shoved his hand into a pocket. Lydia gave Simon a quick kiss and now they were looking at him expectantly.

"This is difficult for everyone connected to your daughter. Do you mind if we chat for a few minutes?"

Simon grunted while his face tightened. Lydia cleared her throat. "Why don't you gents get settled and I'll start the coffee." She nodded at Justin, then stepped away in the direction of what he assumed was the kitchen. Simon stared after her for a moment.

"Well, let's have a seat in the living room." He finally pointed with his chin, and led the way to a room with leather and plush furniture and a sizeable tropical aquarium. If Simon needed counselling, he would hire expensive professionals. This wouldn't be a long meeting.

"I - we, at Rendel care about Annie very much." He emphasized by moving both hands while he spoke. "I wanted to drop by today to let you know that we have several services for students and parents who are feeling her absence." He handed over his business card. "You'll find the information on our website and my direct line is on the card if you have any questions. We want you to know we're here for you."

Simon studied the card. "Okay." He swallowed. "Anything else?"

Wow, wrapping up the conversation already. "Simon, this is a confusing and emotional time. It's very important for you to speak your feelings and ideas with professionals or loved ones around you. Do you have a support network?"

"I have friends, sure. And my wife." His jaw set.

"That's good, that's good. I'm sorry that you're going through this." *And I wish your wife were beside you supporting your connection with Annie's school.* He wanted to say that, but it wasn't his place. "I'm going to wrap things up, but I also brought something for you in case you aren't able to get the support you need from our services or elsewhere." He pulled out a small pamphlet. "This is some information about local churches. Sometimes the atmosphere can bring hope to those going through hard circumstances, even if you're not religious yourself." Simon took it, and briefly looked at the cover before setting it down beside him. The fish tank hummed and a purple tropical blur made a sudden dive, sending up a flurry of bubbles. "I also work with youth at a nearby church. Cadence Rhode attends the group and mentioned that she plays on the same soccer team as Annie."

Simon's expression noted Cadence's name. He nodded.

"Annie has stopped by our church a couple times too."

This time Simon's eyebrows raised in surprise. "Well, I don't know too much about any of that, but -" He lifted Justin's business card and studied it again. "Thank you to your church for caring about Annie. Here -" He reached into his wallet and withdrew his own business card. "You can call if you want to check in on the investigation."

Justin reached forward and took the card. "I will, thank you. I won't take any more of your time. Remember, if you need someone to talk to, or just a place to go where you can think, we're here for you.

Drop by or give me a call." He reached forward and took Simon's hand in a firm shake. "I'll see myself out."

At least both parents made an appearance here. At the Fischer house, Teagan's father hadn't been heard from all day.

Chapter 6

"What - are you going to try something?" Ryan scrunched his brows for appearance but nearly broke into a grin. These teenage-bravery games were amusing and ridiculous. Her whole body looked tense and he could have called her move from across a field. Had she learned nothing from his 'surprise attack' training on the team or from yesterday's events? "Really?"

She sighed loudly and collapsed back into her chair. "Yeah," she threw up a hand. "I thought I could, I don't know, beat you somehow and get away." She met his eyes and suddenly looked afraid.

"Give me a break, kid. But thanks for your honesty. Come on, eat the sandwich." He faked concentration towards his phone, but kept his peripheral vision on her. She wasn't as reckless as Teagan, which was good, but she was quick-witted, and that in a way required more attention. She'd always respected his authority though and that came with some reward, even as a hostage.

"Wait, you're not mad at me? I'm not in trouble?"

He looked at her, then back at his phone. "You're a smart girl and you know better than to take me on in a fight. If I catch you again though, I'll break your nose. Now eat your food before I take it away." Mind games again; he wouldn't ever actually hit her. Only criminals hit women. He glanced up as she reached for the sandwich and carefully sniffed it. "It's safe."

She glanced up and he looked back at his phone.

"Can't feed you drugs every day." A moment passed by. She cleared her throat and he noticed the food still untouched in her hand. "You're not hungry or what?" He raised an eyebrow. "I'm going to eat that if you don't."

"How much longer do we have to stay here, Coach -" She shook her head. "I mean, *Ryan*."

He lowered his phone and contemplated. If he told her the truth, he risked having her close up emotionally and that wouldn't be good for anyone. "We'll see." He settled in a tone that stated there was nothing else to say on the matter. His phone wasn't getting service down here, but he looked at it again anyway to give them both space.

"What about nationals next month?" She looked up from her sandwich again, "Teagan's the striker and the team needs me on defence. This is affecting everybody!"

Naive thinking again. He'd considered this in the weeks leading up to the kidnapping. After all, he hardly had a personal life outside of the team. Ideally the timing would have been better suited a few weeks from now, but his new love interest had changed everything. The relationship was destructive, but it also made him feel good, which took a lot for someone like him. He shook his head and adjusted his dark cap.

"The team will make things work. Everyone is replaceable, Annie." The jab wasn't meant for her, he thought, as he saw pain on her face, nor was it true. She was a fantastic player and the season was over without her and Teagan, but the sooner kids accepted the world would go on without them, the better off they'd be. He ignored her stare. His thoughts were actually on the boy he had come to call a brother a long time ago. One of the many his parents had abducted during his childhood. They had let Cole stay alive for a couple years, unlike the other boys, because he was great at chopping wood and helping with other chores. Ryan had allowed himself to form a bond with Cole, which was something he'd never done before, and hadn't tried again since. Except for Michelle. But Cole had talked back to Ryan's dad one evening and that had changed everything. Afterward, as Ryan helped bury him in the yard, his father had said those same words to him:

"Everyone is replaceable. Let it go."

He'd been sixteen at the time. Until that point he had no idea who he was or how he fit into society as the son of vagabond killers. He'd been forced to live a double life and cover the abuse with a created

66

personality for the few years he'd been allowed to go to school as a child. He was threatened with the lives of the other boys if he ever told the police. However, despite his efforts to protect them, all the other boys were eventually buried too.

But from that day on he had begun strength training so one day he would be strong enough to fend off his father and create a life of his own. His new habits hadn't gone unnoticed though and his father began inviting a man to their home. A disgusting man who would force Ryan outside in the night and take him far into the back yard to a shed. But Ryan had refused to be broken. He'd continued to train hard and make plans for his future. A few weeks after his eighteenth birthday the opportunity came.

The pedophile got drunk with his parents one night, before grabbing Ryan by the collar and pushing him out into the yard. As they made their way to the shed Ryan felt the man sway with each step and even stagger once. As soon as he was shoved into the small building he lunged for a garden hoe and swung it at the man's head. The man stumbled forward from the force and crashed against a shelf of smaller tools before falling to the ground. Ryan had stood stunned for several minutes before checking for a pulse. He was dead. Ryan hadn't even moved away from the body when his father barged into the shed demanding to know what the ruckus was about. Ryan lunged at him before he could register what had happened. After about a minute his father lay unconscious on the floor. His mother came out about fifteen minutes later to see what was keeping his father out so long. She was the hardest to take down, not because of her strength, but because she was afraid of him. And she cried when he took hold of her arms to keep her from beating his chest with her fists while she screamed up at him. Eventually she'd slid to the floor and Ryan let go, trying to think of how he could keep her contained without hurting her. But then she'd reached beneath a shelf and pulled out a gun. Instinct kicked in and he'd knocked her out.

There hadn't been other children on the acreage at that time, which meant he could escape on his own and finally be free. But the realization of what he'd done began to fill his mind with fear. He'd have to go to the police...and convince them he couldn't stop his parents from killing the children buried on the yard. No one would believe him. And he'd just murdered a man. The freedom he'd longed for his entire life would end with him in a jail cell.

He'd bound his parent's hands and feet, and dragged the three bodies into a cellar on the yard. At that point his fear had overwhelmed his mind past the point of reason - now he wanted control. By the end of that night they all had his initials carved into their skin. He watched them die slowly and carved new cuts when -

"- an. Ryan?" Annie's voice pierced his thoughts. He shook his head and blinked several times. The past was a dangerous place to get lost, especially in the presence of other people. His chest rose and fell as he pressed his lips together and let the memories go. He noticed her food still untouched in her hand

"Okay, Annie -" His irritation was sounding sharper than he meant it to, "If you don't eat that -" She quickly brought it to her mouth and took a bite. He stopped talking, sighed and rolled his shoulders, then cracked his neck.

"What were you thinking about?" She asked between chews. Her dirty blonde hair draped innocently over her shoulders.

"You're asking a lot of questions today", he warned, looking away. She'd always been intuitive, and that was not something he needed today. Especially from a teenager. He repositioned his legs and looked at his dead phone again.

"Sorry." She looked away for a moment before helping herself to the water bottle. He wanted to demand that she speak her words clearly or not at all and to look him in the eyes while talking. But instead he dropped his elbows to his knees and diverted his stare to the side of the room.

Way too much thinking today, he counselled. *Probably a wise idea to run another five kilometers to clear your mind.*

"I've just never seen you like -"

"Okay, kid -" He stood and snatched the bread and bottle away, tossing them onto the table. "You're done in here." He grabbed the tape and narrowed his brows at her as she stared back with childish wet eyes. He yanked both her hands behind her back and started taping them together. Unbelievably though, she continued to speak.

"I think I look like that when I remember my mom. Angry, alone...confused."

He ripped the end of the tape, and pressed her hands together firmly. Then circled to the front. "Something bad happened to you, Ryan. I've seen it in your eyes since last year. Cadence said her God can help us heal." She was looking straight up at him, as if she could still trust him with her thoughts and questions. His stomach knotted uncomfortably.

"I don't want to hear about it." He plastered tape across her mouth, then lifted her to standing position by the arm and pulled her to the door.

"MMM!" Her arm slipped from his grasp as she pulled away.

"What now?" He nearly yelled. Her brown eyes were wide and wet. *Come on...* He ripped the tape off her mouth.

"Ah, ow!" She dropped her head. "You grabbed my bandages and the cuts still hurt."

He stooped down to look her right in the eyes. "Well, the next time I ask you to do something, don't make me ask it again. Got it?" He flattened the tape back over her mouth, then slid his bag from his shoulders and carefully unwrapped the bandages to check for infection. He poured a small amount of peroxide on one section of skin. She squeezed her eyes shut in pain and, despite her attempts, a sharp, muffled cry escaped from her covered mouth. The sound made his stomach twist again. He needed to get outside and run *now*. These emotions were messing with his mind.

But Teagan still needed to eat. Or he could let her starve because frankly, he hadn't let her escape attempt go, mostly because of what it had pushed him to do. He'd laid awake most of the previous

70

night hearing Annie's screams in his mind. The reasoning that finally allowed rest was: if he'd punished Teagan she would have taken the pain, and probably done it again, but she'd probably behave if Annie had to take the consequences for her actions. But what he'd done was not wise, not human. His anger had taken over and he didn't realize he'd lost control until he was halfway home. And hearing Teagan's lippy attitude again this morning made him wonder if he'd been wrong her.

Yes, she could easily pull another stupid move. So torturing Annie had been pointless.

"Oh, do you still need the washroom?" He glanced down at Annie and she nodded. He slipped his knife between her wrists. "Make it quick." He watched her hurry across the room, away from her abuser. It wasn't supposed to be like this. He was a coach. A life changer. A mentor. And yet he'd wounded her with his own hands. Torture wasn't supposed to follow him here. He'd killed it a long time ago and buried it so that it'd never be found again. He leaned against the doorframe.

Annie didn't even ask for an apology.

No, she'd tried to reach into his heavy, dirty mind. A place he'd vowed never to open to another soul again. She'd been kind, even after he'd cut and drugged her yesterday. If his parents could see what he'd done, they would probably tell him they were proud. That he'd turned out just like them. He swallowed and dropped his head for a moment. When he looked up Teagan was staring at him, jaunty and bold. But also, helpless and afraid. Her glassy eyes held different fear than the kind he saw and appreciated as her coach.

But this was different from what his parents had done with their hostages! They'd kidnapped children for their own selfish gain, while he on the other hand, had brought Annie and Teagan here to protect them. But they didn't know that yet and he couldn't possibly explain the situation now. It was too complex for young girls to understand. Especially Annie. When the time was right he would explain everything, but all they needed to know right now was that he was in charge, and there had to be rules to build a structured future.

Yes, he looked like the bad guy because of how rough he was on them. But if he went easy they wouldn't take the danger seriously. Perhaps things would stop being so emotional once they understood. Then they would thank him.

He would be a hero.

Annie crossed the room and sat down. She leaned her head against Teagan's shoulder and closed her eyes.

Don't you dare fall apart in front of me! I'm doing this to keep you alive...

He cut Teagan's legs free.

"Get up and use the washroom, and then I have something for you to eat." She was cooperative apart from her defiant glare. But as he locked the door afterwards, the image of them leaning against each other with tears on their faces made an unmoving imprint on his mind and weighed like bricks on his chest.

Damn you, kids.

He ran another thirteen kilometers.

Chapter 7

God? Can you hear me? Cadence says you're real. She says you see everything.

Annie leaned against the cold wall with a thin blanket from Ryan draped over her. He'd left about half an hour ago without any promises to come back later. The light that usually shone under the door from the next room was gone so there weren't any shadows now. Only endless darkness. Teagan lay across her lap awkwardly and her rhythmic breathing signalled that she had fallen asleep.

God, we need your help. Ryan needs your help too...this isn't like him. Maybe if you send someone to talk to him...

Water dripped in the bathroom. Drip, drip, drip.

I'm so hungry and cold. And scared.

She closed her eyes and leaned her head against the cold wall. *Please help us.*

***

"These are fantastic." Michelle smiled as she scrolled through Ryan's pictures. "Oh, this design on Teagan's arm must've taken some time, it's so intricate. It almost looks like a rose." She sipped at her dark roast coffee from one of his brown mugs.

"I thought you'd like it." Patterns from Aztec art had fascinated him since he was a child and he'd created beautiful pieces on wood, metal and other surfaces in his lifetime. Though this was only the second time other humans were involved. He wiped sleep away from his eyes. "I told you I can carve you something even lovelier than that on wood."

She glanced up from his phone. "Anyone can craft on wood, babe. Your skin designs are unique."

He cracked his neck and was silent a moment. "Well, they've got small bodies. I'll run out of space eventually." *And It's draining me.*

"We'll figure something else out when you do. You're not trying to get out of this, are you?" More coffee.

He studied the top of her downturned head and swallowed. "No."

"Because that was our deal: We'll let them live if you can prove to me that they're suffering. By the way, it'd be great if you could get more of their faces in the shots, especially Annie's. I'd love to see some tears, you know?"

"They're drugged when I'm working, it's not like they're posing for me."

She shot him a dangerous look that said *'Get it done'*.

He crossed his arms. "I was thinking maybe I could come up with a better method. I mean, I don't personally have anything against these girls. Scars and blood are a bit dark."

"I got the idea from you", she retorted. She moved her eyes sideways as she swiped to the next picture.

"Yeah, but I did it the first time for survival and revenge I guess, this time is -"

"Revenge is the whole reason for this!" Her eyes blazed. Jada bounded into the kitchen and barked up ay Michelle's lap. "You do as I say or I'm putting a pistol to their heads."

"Jada, back!" He snapped his fingers at the ground, but Jada continued howling up at Michelle's intense tone.

Michelle ignored her. "If you're thinking of going to the police, just remember: You share my secret, then I'll share yours."

He set his jaw. If he didn't think she'd pull out her gun and do exactly as she said, he'd push the topic further, but he wanted to play it safe. "I need to hit the shower. Leave my phone on the table when you're done." He got up from the table and pecked her forehead with a kiss.

"I'd say so. How much running did you do today?"

"Not enough." He disappeared into the hallway and punched a closet door on his way to the washroom.

***

12:30PM

Simon drove into the neighbourhood he'd been in only one other time. It had been for a celebratory barbeque when the girls brought home gold from nationals last year. Soccer was still all Annie talked about, and with five practices a week, her coach probably saw more of her than he did. Besides himself, Ryan Grey was likely the most influential person in Annie's life. What did he expect to gain from this visit? Perhaps a listening ear or maybe even a friend who would understand how he felt. He pulled up to the curb a few houses away and parked. He looked himself over in the rear-view mirror and sighed.

Well, here goes nothing.

He got out of his truck and ambled towards the relatively new cedar steps leading up to the door. He pressed the doorbell and slipped his hands inside his light jacket. Immediately a dog began barking and the volume increased as the dog ran up to the other side of the door. A shrill whistle sounded and the barking stopped. A moment later the door opened.

"Hello, Coach Grey." Simon extended his hand immediately. The young man looked stunned for a moment, but then took Simon's hand. A minty scent from his skin and wet hair signalled a recent shower. "Sorry for disturbing you, I just wanted to stop by for a minute to - I mean, how are you doing, Coach Grey?" He stumbled awkwardly. With all the credit Annie gave to her coach, Simon felt awful that he couldn't piece together a simple conversation with him.

"You can just call me, 'Ryan'. I'm fine, and you?" Ryan's eyes darted away and looked like they couldn't find a place to settle. Simon didn't blame him for being uncomfortable. A troubled father whom he barely knew had shown up on his doorstep unannounced.

"I was driving and, well, looking for a friend, I suppose. Someone else who would be missing Annie." He stuffed his hands back into his coat and offered a weak smile.

"Of course, sir. I can't imagine what you must be feeling." Ryan stepped out and pulled the door closed behind him as his dog tried to push through. He crossed his arms and narrowed his brown eyes to chow concern.

"Well, actually, I thought you might understand a little bit. This must put a strain on your team with nationals approaching. That's all Annie's talked about for the last few weeks."

"Yes, it's been tough on the team." He scratched the back of his neck and nodded.

Simon broke eye contact and studied the cedar steps. "You and I don't know one another, Ryan, but I hear your name so often it's

almost like you're part of our family. Annie speaks so highly of you."
He looked back and gave an embarrassed smirk. "You probably think
I'm crazy, blubbering on like this." He forced a chuckle.

"Not at all, sir. This is extremely difficult for all of us. If I can
do anything to help, please call me anytime." He took Simon's hand
again in a firm shake. "I'm sorry to cut this short, but I've got a client
at the gym right away."

"Oh! I'll let you go then, thank you for the chat, son. Likewise,
please feel free to call me if you need to chat...or anything." He waited
for Ryan to nod, then turned to head back down the stairs and heard the
door close behind him.

*That went alright. Once Annie is home I'll have to see if he has
a girlfriend he can bring over for dinner one day.*

***

1:30 PM

Ryan dropped his gym bag by the weights and took a long swig
from his water bottle. The unplanned visit from Simon had sent his
mind reeling but luckily, he kept his composure until Simon had left.
His legs had nearly buckled under his nerves afterwards, as he slid to
the floor in his home. Had Simon come over five minutes sooner while
Michelle was still there, the whole plan would have gone South. And

what had Simon said? That he viewed him as *'family'*? That was absurd. There couldn't be anything farther from the truth.

Unless... what if Simon had figured him out and was trying to get into his head? Music cranked from a speaker nearby and he shook his head. Simon's a doctor, but if he hadn't noticed his daughter emotionally slipping away for months he couldn't have figured out Ryan's involvement in her disappearance.

Better pray that Michelle doesn't find out about all this though! As if a prayer could save him. Who knows what kind of crazy evil she'd do if she got the slightest inkling that he'd screwed up. She'd fight every inch of detail out of his brain and probably kill him, regardless of what he told her. He swung his arms in rotations around his gray t-shirt and began rotating his core. But the conversation with Simon had been concise and he'd cut it short with a legitimate excuse. No secrets were shared. He planted his blue Adidas runners in front of him and dropped into the first in a series of lunges. Ignoring Simon would have looked suspicious, but he'd been discreet and done what was socially acceptable and shown respect to him. No one would question why he was speaking with a worried father.

A father who'd lost a child. Like Cole's father. And Lucas's father. And Benjie's father. And -

He nearly hurled the weight bench across the room.

Don't do this! You're in a safe place now. You don't have to take your mind back there.

After a slow exhale, he jumped into high knee tucks. Self-coaching to the rescue again. Blood rushed, transmitting healthy endorphins from his brain. He'd beaten his past and the bravery and vigor that brought him to the present would carry him forward. He finished the set and breathed heavily. As he grabbed his water bottle he noticed a middle-aged man appear near the entrance, seemingly looking for someone.

"Spencer?" Ryan called. The man noticed him and raised his eyebrows with a nod. He carried a large duffel over his wide shoulders and broad chest.

"Wade Spencer." He introduced as he made his way around numerous pieces of exercise equipment and several other people. He dropped his gym bag on a weight bench. "You must be Ryan Grey?"

"You bet." Ryan took his hand in a firm shake. "You found this place alright?"

"Oh, yeah. Been contemplating joining this gym for months, just needed the right motivation. That's what I'm paying you for." He grinned and his gaze ran down Ryan's body, then back up. Sizing him up as a trainer, perhaps. It was odd, but not the strangest thing that had happened to him when meeting a client for the first time. Once an older gentleman had requested that he attend Thanksgiving dinner at his home in place of their son, who was about Ryan's age and couldn't fly home for the holiday.

"You got it." He allowed a partial grin in return. "We'll do an hour set today like we discussed. You can pay at the front when we're done."

"Let's get started!" Beginner's elation.

You're gonna hate me soon. But you'll thank me for the results later.

"You said quads, correct?" Ryan squirted water to his mouth then set the bottle aside.

"That'd be great." Wade peeled off the jacket and tossed it onto his bag. His large arms flexed with his movements.

"Alright. You stretched before you came?"

"Yeah, man", he laughed easily. "Not going to pay you to watch me stretch."

"Good, and I won't pay for your hospital bill if you tell me you stretched when you haven't. Sound fair?" It sounded unprofessional. He wasn't talking to a team of teenagers. His mouth needed his mind to be in the present. "It's important, that's all."

"I got it, man! This isn't my first rodeo." He smiled wide. Creases that showed age, perhaps fifteen years Ryan's senior, led up his face.

"Okay, great. We'll do reps with heavy weights first. How much do you normally lift?"

"About forty per side." Ryan lifted thirty-five. This man had maintained his stamina despite his age. Impressive. He obviously valued fitness and clients like these excelled with Ryan's training.

"We'll start at twenty-five per side with squats. Have your legs shoulder-width a part. Yeah, that looks good." Ryan began to grab weights and slide them onto the bar. "It's good to start with less than you're used to", he explained. "Let's see how many reps you do comfortably."

"Sounds good to me." Wade shook his pale arms as he rolled his large neck.

"Alright, because you want this bar above your shoulders you're going to want to lift like this first -" Ryan motioned for him to step back to make space. He demonstrated by lifting the weights in front, and transferring them back to the shoulders. "Got it? Okay, can you give me five reps?"

"Sure thing, bro." His grin hinted that he was talking down to Ryan. That's fine. He was entitled to his opinion. And if he wanted him as a coach he'd feel pain in places he didn't know could hurt. The disrespect would end after their first session. It usually did. He watched Wade's body as he began to lift.

"Hold on, lift with your knees and arch your back like I did." He rested one hand on his hip and watched Wade's body move. "There, good. Again. Four more." He studied Wade's legs and back as he completed the set.

Wade dropped the weights and blood pumped, blushing his face. "Easy!" He grinned and shook his arms.

"Good." Ryan nodded. "How's your back?"

"I feel good." He hopped on the toes of his black shoes before twisting his torso from side to side.

Ryan cracked his knuckles. "Alright, Spencer, give me another five. Let's go."

"You got it, man." Wade rolled his shoulders, then anchored his stance and lifted.

"Stop, you'll pull out your back if you lift like that. Remember, from your knees." Wade grunted and lowered the weights. "Start again. That's better. Good." He was catching on. "Form will make or break you. There you go. Two left. Good, make this last one count."

He lifted, then lowered the weights with a crimson color in his cheeks. He let out a low whistle. "Wow, what a ride!" He grinned and ran a large hand over his short-cropped hair.

"Good work." Ryan nodded and grabbed his bottle, then reached for Wade's and tossed it to him.

"Thanks, bro, this is great." Both men drank. "I'm glad I found you." He tossed his bottle and rolled his shoulders again. Ryan watched him loosen his muscles.

"One minute, then I want five more."

Wade grinned between torso twists. "Now I see what signed up for." Respect. It was starting to show. "You've come a long way, you know." Wade was stretching his arms across his chest now.

"I'm sorry?" Ryan raised his brows and turned his head in question. He squirted in another swallow.

"I said, you've really made something of yourself, *Rylan*."

Ryan choked and nearly spit his water on the floor. He began coughing to clear his throat. Wade dropped his arms, and a frightening smugness colored his face.

"What? People don't call you that anymore?"

Ryan pounded his chest with his fist and his throat cleared below his reddening cheeks. Rylan. *Rylan.* That was almost thirteen years ago, from the life when he lived as a prisoner in his own home. After he got away he'd left everything behind, including his name. Contacts from previous homes forged the new identity. *Rylan Grede,* the victim, had died with his parents. But apparently not everything had stayed buried.

"Bet you didn't think your old life would catch up to you." A dangerous glare accompanied his words.

"Who are you?" Ryan demanded through clenched teeth.

"I'm your past, baby! And I know what you did." He sneered. *But how could he know?*

His parents rarely stayed anywhere long enough to make connections. Unless Wade had known the pedophile... "Word on the street says you work with teenage girls?" He slapped Ryan's shoulder and let out a harsh laugh. "The apple doesn't fall far from the tree."

"Get your hands off me." He shoved him away. "What do you want?" The conversation ignited a long-hidden fire of rage. Although it would make for a good fight, a few more words and he'd come undone and lose the respect he'd built for himself.

"Same thing everyone wants, bro. Money." He scoffed at the look of anger and defeat in Ryan's eyes and cracked his neck again.

"You're not getting anything from me."

"He liked you, you know? James did. He'd tell me stories about '*the boy, named Rylan*'. Said you were 'beautiful'." He winked.

Ryan stepped forward fast. "Say that again." His fists clenched at his side.

"I see what he meant. You've got spunk too and I like that."

Ryan tried to push down the anger rising in his throat. Wade's dark eyes didn't move and his lips curled, daring Ryan to break. A young woman who had been lifting dumbbells nearby grabbed her water bottle and left the area quickly. "Get out." He growled.

"James was my brother", Wade continued. "My younger brother. He had a picture of you in his truck that he'd look at every morning." His voice darkened. "A day hasn't passed where I didn't study it and break my body in training so I could rip you apart with my own hands. And now, here you are. Grown up and alone. Or maybe you have more corpses hiding in your closet."

"You don't know what you're talking about", he shot back, noticing a few more concerned patrons moving away from the conflict. He cleared his throat again and lowered his voice. This was a place where people respected him and he didn't want to lose that. "Get out of my gym."

"And what? Out of your life? No way, baby boy, I'm here to stay." His smirk widened as Ryan reacted to his words. "Oh, you don't

86

like that? Thought once you got rid of them that all the bad things would go away?"

Ryan noticed that his legs had started to shake. Nausea and heat were spreading through his body.

"Not in this lifetime, pretty boy." He cracked his knuckles. "You're going to pay for what you did." He glared down with deadly eyes, then stepped back and shouldered his gym bag. "You'll hear from me."

Cold sweat drenched Ryan's hair and t-shirt as he watched him walk away.

***

3:30 PM

Ryan threw the black bag of soccer balls over his back and slammed his jeep hatch shut. The second unwanted visit today had twisted his stomach like a towel and he'd barely made it to the gym restroom in time to throw up.

A sing-song inner voice taunted: *Somebody knows your secret.*

He was trapped again.

NO! A second voice insisted. *You've become more than helpless!*

Yes, he mused, he'd escaped on his own against all odds. He'd brought justice to Cole, and all the other murdered children and there'd be no more killing on that farm because he'd stopped the killers.

But once the authorities come for you it will all be over! And Michelle will kill Annie and Teagan. You'll never be strong enough to protect anyone!

He stopped at the edge of the field and flung the bag. A few balls rolled out and he pulled a pen out of his windbreaker to take attendance.

"Hey, Coach!"

He jumped as a couple girls ran past and giggled at his reaction. "Hey, ladies." Check. Check. The pen shook in his hand. *Pull yourself together, Ryan!* A cool breeze brushed his neck and he instinctively slapped at the itch it caused. "Colts, don't drag your feet! You'll destroy your cleats."

"Yes, Coach!" She called over her shoulder. On the field he demanded respect, commitment and good sportsmanship - but he'd caused the slow and painful death of his own mother! And kidnapped their friends. What kind of hypocrite did that make him?

A criminal one.

You should be locked behind bars for life for your crimes!

But I had to do it! He argued mentally. *I'd tried everything else.* He really had. Once when he was twelve, his school teacher had asked about the bruises and scars on his arms because he had taken off his sweater during class. He'd burst into tears and told her what his parents

88

did. A cop had driven him home that day. But his parents were the perfect con-artists and while his dad sweet-talked the cop, his mom hid the young boys in a cellar beneath one of the sheds. They hugged Ryan repeatedly in front of the officer and said he'd fallen out of a tree and was prone to wild stories. When the officer left his dad had shot one of the boys and made sure Ryan knew it was his fault. Then his mom whipped him where his female teacher would never look. They'd moved away shortly after that. As he'd gotten older he'd tried different ways to talk to authorities or escape, but every attempt had brought similar results and consequences.

"Hey, Coach!" This time he nearly shouted from shock. Cadence Rhodes. He closed his eyes for a moment to catch his breath and search for extra patience he knew he didn't have. She was a well-rounded teen, but also very intuitive, and that was still not something he needed. If she caught the slightest hint that he was at odds, there would be no stopping her sensitivity from reaching inside his mind and revealing something. He tried to swallow but his throat was very dry.

"Rhodes." He noted her presence without looking at her, hoping that she'd keep moving. But today was not a day of luck for him.

"I want to share something with you, like something related to last practice!" Her voice bubbled with enthusiasm.

"How about you just get out there and stretch?" He looked back at the field and continued with attendance. An image of his duct-tape flashed across his mind.

"But, I just feel in my heart that God wants me to pray for Annie and Teagan's kidnapper."

He almost choked on her innocence but covered his mouth with a sleeve and coughed. *No need to get riled up - that whole religion thing is a hoax anyway.* He scratched his neck and looked back at the field for other players. But he couldn't even concentrate because she was still staring up at him. *Don't do this, Rhodes.*

"I feel..." She continued, "that whoever has them is struggling inside with a deep wound... something from their past. I feel that they need to know that Jesus can set them free." Her eyes glittered and he nearly yelled at her for getting inside his head.

Stop preaching at me!

He repositioned his cap and looked back at his clipboard. "I don't see you stretching", he snapped. She had a gift, he'd give her that, and she'd probably grow up to be some crazy psychologist or psychic. But today he needed her out of his head. He closed his eyes, thankful for the shadow his cap provided.

"But Coach -"

"Stretching or push-ups, Rhodes!"

"Yes, Coach!" She jogged out and spun back. "I just have a feeling that everything is going to work out!" She grinned and sprinted to where Colts and a few others girls were warming up. Ryan sighed and scratched the back of his neck. These girls all had great potential and he was the one training them, pushing them, helping them become better. He was giving back to the community and molding respect and good behaviour into their young lives. His character had stood as an exemplary role model and parents and community members had told him so.

But his sins were back to destroy everything he'd worked for.

Where were people like Cadence when he was a hostage in his own home? People who somehow tapped into a higher power and knew things that no one else did. The thoughts hovered for a moment, but then he shook his head. That would mean he believed a god existed. Which wasn't true. No one could have saved him and no one who could interfere with his actions now.

"Teen naivety for the win again." Great, now he was talking to himself.

But how did she know?

Chapter 8

Wade Spencer watched Rylan yelling instructions at his team and shook his head. The man didn't even know half the story of his own identity and here he was trying to tell these girls who they needed to be? Pathetic, that's what this boy was.

Rylan wouldn't remember him, but Wade had worked closely with his parents for years. He took unhappy boys and traded them for goods or cash at isolated locations. His brother, James had just been a third party to it all and was only brought in to teach this stupid kid some discipline and respect. He had no other reason to be involved. But Rylan couldn't be broken, no matter how often James took him. And then one day they all disappeared. Don, Lois, James, and Rylan. Was it a coincidence? Of course not, and they hadn't ridden off into the sunset either. Rylan had killed them. He was sure of it, especially after seeing the look in his eyes today.

This floundering youth owed him his life. Three lives actually. Wade spat sideways as he saw Rylan collect his things as practice ended. Today was payday. And Rylan would pay for his crimes one way or another.

***

Ryan tossed the bag of balls into his jeep with one hand. The hatch looked like a storm had passed through and his OCD nature made him cringe. *One thing at a time.* He'd been told once that starting a second task before finishing the first caused brain dysfunction. There was probably truth to that because his mind had been twisted in several directions today and he was beyond a migraine. He rubbed his aching head and instinctively removed his cap and shook off the sweat beads. What a day. And it wasn't finished. Annie and Teagan needed to eat, which meant another drive to the forest and jog to the bunker. Jada needed to eat too. And he was starving. Nausea began to wrap around him like a hot blanket. Perhaps calling a cab to get home would be a better idea than driving.

Get your act together! His mind screamed. *You're falling apart.*

I'm doing my best with what I have to work with! He mentally shouted back.

He ran his hand ran along his forehead and let his heavy eyes close for a moment. A crying face flashed across his mind. A little boy. He berated himself for allowing the thought. Windows to the past needed to stay closed. That's the reason it's called 'the past'. It's over. Finished. Beaten. He scrunched his eyes and the image vanished. But then another young boy appeared, this one wearing a blue cotton sweater.

"Rylan? Where is my family? Why can't I see my mom?"

No! That's the past! It had no right to follow him here. He pressed the bridge of his nose hard and pain spread up his forehead from his clenched eyes. Another freckled face with a contagious grin. Cole.

"Rylan, want to build a fort? Rylan, want to go to the stream together? Rylan, help me! Help -"

He opened his eyes and realized they were wet. He swallowed and images continued to play. Cole screaming at him, but not being able to do anything because his dad had busted Ryan's arm and tied him to a tree so he wouldn't interfere.

"I won't it again! I promise! Rylan, help me! Ryl-an!"

He closed his eyes and shook his head. *You're broken.* He dropped his chin at the accusation. *You can run, but you'll never heal.* His bottom lip trembled. *'Something happened to you, Ryan. Cadence said her God can help us heal.'* Annie's words. Could that really be possible? He exhaled slowly, holding the hatch door for a moment. He needed rest and clarity, and he desperately needed food. He pulled it shut and took a breath.

"Hi, Rylan."

He spun so quickly he nearly fell over. Wade leaned against the back of the jeep in a black, long-sleeved button down shirt and jeans. He was smoking a cigar.

"Get away from me." Ryan stepped around him to the driver's door.

"Uh, uh." Wade pressed a cold metal object against his ribs. Ryan relaxed back on his footing and licked his lips. A gun.

He grit his teeth and took a shallow breath. "Put that away."

"Listen, pretty boy", he spoke smoothly, "You come with me now or I'll shoot one of your school girls." Ryan followed his gaze and saw Dani, Regine and Layla on their phones about fifty feet away. "You don't want to be the reason another child is killed. Do you?"

He set his jaw. "Don't touch them."

"Oh, this is all up to you, Rylan. You choose if this gets hard or not." His eyes were cold, as though they'd seen death many times. He pushed the barrel of the gun harder against him.

"My name is 'Ryan'." Whatever went down between the two of them couldn't happen here. They needed to go somewhere else. Where no one would witness the violence and whatever terror Wade had in mind. The shed from his childhood flashed like the previous images and he shivered. Wade saw the movement and grinned. Ryan scowled and clenched his fists. "We're not doing this here."

"There! Was that so hard?" Wade laughed casually and slapped Ryan's shoulder. "That's me over there." He referenced a pickup truck across the street. "Have a lovely evening, ladies!" He called to the young trio. Their heads spun to the stranger. Ryan had taught them to respect every individual on the field, especially coaches and parents from other teams. He also warned them about speaking with people they didn't know. It wasn't part of his job, but it had come up at practise, and parents didn't seem to mind the extra lessons.

Dani spoke first, but it wasn't her fault; Ryan was with the stranger. "Uh, you too, sir! Night, Coach!" Regine and Layla echoed their respects. Ryan looked away, hoping that would be signal enough not to trust this man. Wade pushed him forward by the shoulder. He didn't know that the exchange would have seemed odd for the girls. That Ryan would have been courteous to their remarks and taunted them with a one-liner. Before he could think twice, his mind sent up a plea: *God, please protect them.* He blinked in shock.

"Get in." Wade ordered.

No time to ponder the prayer.

A prayer? He had prayed?

"I said, get in." Wade shoved him against the truck. Ryan jerked away. "I heard you." He reached for the door latch and felt Wade's breath on his neck.

"Think about what's at stake if you try anything, pretty."

Ryan opened the door and climbed in without looking back.

"There we go. Now you see this?" He stuffed the gun into his jeans. "I'm a quick draw and it's staying on me." He slammed the door. Ryan scanned the windshield, looking for the girls. But they were gone. He let out a breath. Had his prayer worked? It may have been a coincidence that they left. Yeah, he didn't even know who a prayer would go to.

Don't kid yourself. There's nothing else out there!

The jab hurt somehow. Was it that absurd to call on something other people put their faith in? Ludicrous, actually. Of all the concepts he refused to acknowledge, religion was at the top of his list. Life was too short to take chances on a god you couldn't see. But today his rattled mind had gone there and he felt ashamed for it. Any more stress and his brain might crack. Wade swung the driver's door open.

"Lovely evening for a drive." He cracked his knuckles. Then loosened his large neck and shoulders for show.

"I don't have money." Ryan repeated his statement from earlier. He'd have money soon, but Wade could never know about that, because he'd flaunt the information, along with whatever he suspected he was guilty of. But things were not as they seemed! He wasn't the criminal an abduction story would portray. Yes, he had done it, but Annie and Teagan would be dead if he hadn't.

He was saving their lives.

But who knows that? You. Michelle. Her brother. Which one of them do you think is going to back your story?

You don't stand a chance in hell when the story gets out.

Another layer of his created world crumbled. Victimized 'Rylan' was coming back.

Wade climbed in and slammed the door. He adjusted the mirrors and the A/C. "No money, hey? That's fine." He cracked his neck again. "Maybe you'll have something else to say about that when I'm done with you." Ryan's pulse spiked and heat spread down his back. How could he get out of this? Nobody would miss him tonight if he didn't come home. Except Jada. Over a decade of building his future, and not one person to call family. His jaw muscles bulged. He might not outlive the night.

***

They'd been driving in silence for forty-five minutes when the truck veered off down a rough dirt road. Blue and pink hues lit the sky above a scattered farming community.

"Just about there." Wade glanced sideways and winked. A couple gold rings wrapped around the fingers that flexed on the steering wheel. They turned off the road and began down a long driveway that had large sections of brush and dying trees on either side. The yard look abandoned as Wade pulled up to an old barn with peeling red paint. He jammed the truck into park and opened his door without speaking.

Ryan took in what was on the yard: A rusted truck body surrounded by tall grass, a pile of rotting wood, and a barbed-wire pen of sorts, though it was sagging considerably and one side had been torn down. There was also a small house on the lot, made of dying wood and broken windows.

"Get out." Wade hadn't shut his door yet and was watching him. "Didn't bring you out here to look around." He moved to slam the door, but then ducked back. "Oh, and you run - I'll shoot you. You get away from me - I'll go back and shoot up a grocery store. Clear?"

Laying out the rules for a hostage. This was all familiar. "Yeah." Ryan rolled his shoulders and pushed open his door. He'd made the decision during the drive that Wade wouldn't be leaving this yard. Not only did he know secrets, but the risk of him killing an innocent person was too high. But could Ryan kill again? Even if it was to protect himself or future victims again. The last thirteen years had been spent searching for redemption after what he had done. Yes, he'd stopped the plans of murderers, but the cost he still paid was enormous. His mind looking into their dying eyes and memories of infection spreading through their wounds. He had wept for days once they finally passed. He'd become what he hated. A killer.

But that was so long ago. He was a different man now.

"Walk in front of me." Wade pointed with his gun. This was a mistake and the tables needed to turn. Annie and Teagan were alone at the bunker. They needed him. His mind swarmed with useless escape options. The only choice that held hope was if Wade waited until they were in the barn to kill him. Perhaps there would be a chance to fight back.

With what? Your hands?

He set his jaw and started forward with his arms at his side, palms open and facing back so Wade knew he was cooperating. The red sun had turned the sky to various purple and blue streaks. A sunset which would have overlooked his jog to the bunker tonight. He continued into the dim, empty barn. He hadn't even taken a breath when images of the old shed crashed against his unarmed mind. The dirty shelves, dusty floorboards, a window in the back. Smells of old straw and dirt rolled up to meet him. All so similar. He shivered the same way he had when James would hold his shoulders and push him into the dark yard. *'It'll be fun this time. I promise.'* His putrid voice echoed. The barn swelled around him now, bringing him back. Nausea hit him in the gut.

***

Cadence lay on her stomach, homework open in front of her. A blanket with yellow and purple designs covered her bed. Dim light gleamed from her lamp, casting shadows around the room. A few medals hung by her jewellery and posters of athletes decorated the walls. Her muscles still complained from practise today. Coach had pushed them hard, one drill after another. She couldn't remember seeing him so red in the face before. Not only that, but he was on edge the whole time. He'd criticized her so hard that by the end of practise she was in tears.

It's Annie and Teagan's absence, she reasoned. But usually adults brought stability in uncertain times. Looked outside the box for ways to stay proactive. That's what she needed right now. He was the epitome of strength to her and many girls on the team, and yet he seemed to be falling apart right along with them.

She bit into an apple and drew her highlighter across the page. Maybe he missed them in a different way as their coach. To her, they were close friends. Perhaps to him they were more like kids he felt responsible for. She smirked at the thought, but it was true. Teenagers or not, they were still kids in the adult world. School counsellors were available to talk with and she'd taken advantage of that resource. It helped some. They'd pointed out that worrying wouldn't change things and that dwelling on the situation wasn't healthy. She wondered then if Coach had someone to talk with. In times of crisis, who would an adult turn to for stability? She paused from her studies to do the only thing she could think of that would help.

Dear God, I pray that Coach would understand tonight that you are looking out for Him. That you see his pain.

She opened her eyes and gazed out her bedroom window. A dark purple wave washed over the sunset sky.

***

Ryan swayed on weak knees. This was ridiculous - he was made of muscle, with years of fighting under his belt - he had no reason to be afraid. Only an idiot would challenge him in a physical match, and no one had beaten him in a fight since he'd run away from the past. His mind flashed to how both his young guests had attempted to do just that in the last twenty-four hours. *Not helping!* He spat back mentally.

Wade was approaching now with a coil of thick rope.

No. No. *No!* James's words from the past hit him again: *'If I leave you untied, you'll fight me. Then I'll have to hurt you.'* Ryan nearly choked on the rising emotion in his chest.

Wade watched Ryan's eyes and grinned. "Jim said he'd tie your scrawny hands beforehand."

And it was *that* smile that hit Ryan in the chest like bricks. He wavered and stumbled backwards. That smile, that expression, was always there before –

Wade laughed loudly at Ryan's paling face. "Oh-oh, are you afraid, baby boy?"

He scowled and shot his gaze away to where a couple rusting brass wheels leaned against the wooden walls. His bearings crept back but his stomach was churning and that, together with lack of food and sleep, made him weak. "What do you think is going to happen here?"

"Come on, this can be as easy or as hard as you want it to be." Wade held the end of the rope in one hand and walked closer. "You want me to be fast, then you'll cooperate."

Ryan stepped back and bent slightly at the knees, flexing his hands. "Get away from me."

"Look, I deserve payment in one form or another and you in prison just isn't fun for either of us."

Ryan glared. "You're deranged."

"You took my brother from me. Someone has to pay for that", he sneered and stepped closer. Ryan moved accordingly. "Every day I wake up knowing he's gone. You know what that feels like, don't you? Knowing that your little brother is dead: Jacob, Connor..." He paused, "Cole."

"Stop!" Ryan hollered.

"It's not fair, is it?" His voice rose and he kept moving. "When a life is ended unjustly." They were inches apart. Wade licked his lips. "Every day I wonder where I was when you killed him. Every day!"

Ryan hollered and attacked, throwing all his weight against Wade and running him backwards. Wade roared and grabbed onto his shoulders just before he lost footing. Both men went down. Ryan landed on top and shoved Wade's neck to the ground, then started clubbing his jaw with excruciating force, again and again. Wade peeled his bloody lips back into a full smile. He was laughing. He grabbed Ryan's fist and yanked down, twisting into a roll with the momentum. They tumbled twice, crashing against the wooden floor, before Wade's legs wrapped around Ryan's waist. Anger contorted his large features and he hooked beneath Ryan's ribs with his fist. Ryan recoiled and lost his breath for a second.

"You fight like a girl!" He wheezed as he swung up for Wade's neck, but connected with his collar bone. Wade bashed the side of Ryan's face, and slammed him against the floor. Ryan tasted blood as it spewed from his mouth.

"You like that, pretty boy?" Wade spat, hitting him again.

"AAH! Is that all you've?" He caught Wade's attacking arm and jerked him down, smashing his own head up into his nose. Wade swore and blood came gushing out as he faltered. Ryan arched up and threw an uppercut to the chin. Wade's head buckled up and backwards, then Ryan mirrored the cheap jab under the ribcage. Blood flew from Wade's face as he took the hit and fell back. Ryan attacked again but Wade was the stronger man, and grabbed Ryan's arm in a painful twist. Ryan screamed, unable to move for a moment. Finally, he twisted against his arm and rolled out, darting back to his feet. He wiped the blood from his mouth with the back of his hand. He couldn't feel his other arm. Wade, now on his knuckles and knees, snarled from the ground, then spat blood to the side.

"Okay, Rylan." He spat again, chuckling. "Like I said, you've got spunk."

Ryan shifted his weight. He had the upper hand now, a couple more blows to the head could kill this man. But could he kill? *Could he?* He wiped blood from his face just as Wade lurched up and ran into Ryan with a force that toppled him backwards. He landed with a resounding thud as his head contacted the floor. White light flashed, then black. His vision returned just as Wade's rock-hard fist punched his eye, then clubbed his jaw. Ryan coughed up more blood and swore. Another fist to the jaw. White light. Bright white. He grasped aimlessly at the space between them. Wade looked like a black silhouette now, and he peeled back and stood.

"You made this hard, boy." He kicked Ryan in the ribs. More blood splattered out his mouth. He saw color, then shadows.

What was your plan?

He grasped at the floor for an object to throw. Was there any other way for this to end? He managed to roll onto his stomach, groaning, and still grasping for something of substance on the floor. All he saw were shadows. Heat flared behind his face. The girls were going to starve to death without him.

Did you have a plan?

He curled his hands slowly. He had to survive. There had to be some way to get out. He yelled and pushed off the ground into blind oblivion. He received another blow to the side of his face that knocked him a hundred-and-eighty degrees around and he crashed back on his stomach. Redemption road ended here. There would be no more fighting for a better future.

'Cadence's God can help us heal.'

Could that be true? Could it? What did he have to lose now?

Another kick to the stomach. He could barely breathe and the shadows skewed into dark unrecognizable shapes

Please...God...help...

He could barely see through the slits of his eyes, but he kept them open to take defeat like a man. He tried to look up as two black shapes stepped up. One shape moved fast and the darkness took him.

Chapter 9

'Your room better be clean when I get back from my meeting tonight!'

Rachel Fischer gazed out at the dark, twinkling night. Autumn smells pulled through her long hair from the soft window seat. Those were the last words she'd hollered at her daughter. A command. Another warning. Then Teagan had left the house again without taking care of her chores. Trent had hollered his own string of orders at the slammed entrance door and demanded to know why his daughter wasn't spending more time at home. A large part, if not all, of the reason was probably the verbal sparring taking place in their kitchen. Only one of the many fights that had happened last week. Fights that Teagan wanted nothing to do with. Brokenness she'd avoided at all costs. And now she had disappeared. The last memory of home would be of her parents yelling while they both tried to commandeer the ship that was their family life.

A worn out, sinking ship.

Rachel brushed hair away from her face and folded her cold fingers around the golden locket on her neck. "Where are you, baby?"

A gust of scented breeze carried her whisper into the night.

***

Shadows. All around him. Freezing, cold wind blew against his bare arms. He tried to move, but he was tied in place.

"Rylan! Rylan!" Cole's voice. He had to help him!

"NO! Cole! No, dad! Stop -" He pulled at the ropes, but they were securely fastened to the tree trunk.

"Rylan! Help me -"

BANG!

"AH!" He jerked up and light crashed into his vision. White light. "Gah", he gasped, squinting. He groped at the empty air, but could barely lift his arms. Every movement caused a different pain and he could hear himself making small noises of affliction that he couldn't control.

"Hey. It's alright." He heard a low voice in the distance. With it came touches of warmth, also from far away. He tried to reach out to grasp it, but his arms felt like lead. "No, no, just relax. Take it easy."

The words were more crisp now. A male voice. Just beyond his squinting eyes. "You're going to be alright."

"Where am..." He slurred. He squinted but the light flashed brightly at him again. When the bright stars cleared, he could tell someone was touching him and tried to push away the unknown touch, but his arms were still too heavy. The contact grew warmer and accompanied dampness on his arm. He squinted again and the light began to fade to muted colors. Blues, grays, browns. A blurry figure sat in front of him. Ryan closed his eyes and tried again. Only one of his eyes would open.

"You gave me a real scare, Ryan." The man wore a navy sweater. He also had glasses on. A cloth lay in his hand. He sat back as if to give Ryan space. Ryan groaned as he tried to concentrate.

"Wa..." He tried to form Wade's name but couldn't convince his lips to do it. He studied the eyes behind the lenses. *It almost looked like... no...NO!* He somehow lurched backwards and smashed his head against the wall behind him. "Urgh!" Heat exploded and black and red stars of heat zapped through his brain. He tried to lift his hands but failed. He peeked out for a second look at his company.

"Whoa, calm down. You're safe now. I'm here to help you, Ryan."

"Simon?" He croaked. But it couldn't be him.

"Yes, it's just me. I did some First Aid. How are you feeling?" Simon drew his hand over his goatee and watched him with concern. A first-aid kit lay open by Ryan's side, along with an ice pack and a couple bottles of water. Ryan eyed the ice warily. Simon handed it to him, and after a moment of watching Ryan struggle with it, helped lift the ice pack to his face and propped Ryan's arm up with a pillow. He pushed the horn-rimmed glasses further up his nose. "How are you feeling?"

"Where am I?" He managed, noticing his words coming through better now. The ice brought immediate relief to his jaw. He gazed around the room for something recognizable. Framed certificates, an office desk, an old clock - nothing he'd seen before. Perhaps this was inside the old home on the farm yard. Or was he in some kind of nightmare experience? Simon, the man he'd set out to undo, sat in front of him with a medical kit, probably containing scissors, tweezers, and drugs. And Ryan could barely move. Simon must have figured everything out. Maybe he and Wade had met and Simon paid him off to give him a beating, and now the authorities were waiting for him outside this room.

"We're in my home. You're safe now."

Ryan's jaw dropped. He groaned at the pain it caused and shut his mouth. Simon's *home*? He couldn't be here! This was enemy territory. He tried to lunge forward to get away but the sudden movement set off stabbing pains all over his body. He moaned and choked back on emotion. Simon placed his strong hand on Ryan's chest and eased him back down onto the bed.

"It's alright. Take a breath, son." *Son*? A strange title to give to your daughter's captor. He blinked at Simon and searched his face. No signs of aggression. "Here -", Simon offered one of the bottles of water. "You're in shock. Can you try and drink this?"

No way. Thanks, but no thanks, doc. That'd be the day he consciously took a drink from someone bent on revenge. Forget jail, he'd probably wake up at the bottom of a river.

"I'm fine."

"Well if you change your mind, it's right here." He set the bottle back on the bed, within easy arm's reach. "I'm sure you're wondering how you ended up here." Still no signs of anger in his voice or body language. Simon folded his arms over his chest as he continued, "I was out driving a couple hours ago - it helps me to think sometimes. Anyway, my thoughts brought me to the soccer fields where you practise. Annie spends so much of her time out there. I guess I thought I'd feel closer to her."

Ryan stared back blankly. *Where was this conversation going?* His jaw screamed for attention. He applied the ice again and ignored the pain in his arm.

"I drove up and noticed a jeep parked on the other side of the street. I didn't think anything of it at first but as I got closer I saw someone leaning against the driver's door." He wiped his palm across his forehead as if he were breaking a sweat. "I only looked closer because it seemed strange, and then I saw ropes! You were completely tied up, Ryan!" He bulged his eyes with his words.

Wait... Simon had found him at the soccer field?

"I jumped out of my truck to see if the person was alive before dialing 911. I'm a doctor," he reminded, as if to justify his actions. "Then I couldn't believe my eyes when I recognized you!" His eyebrows nearly pushed past his hairline. If Ryan's facial muscles were cooperating they would have shaped complete confusion. *He'd been found at the soccer field?*

"You brought me here..."

Simon nodded and pushed up his glasses again. "I work in emergency and I knew you'd be waiting for hours to get a bed and attention. I figured I could at least get you cleaned up then see if you still wanted to go to the hospital. Besides, like I said to you the other day: You're like family in this home. I know you would have done the same if Annie had been in your place."

His stomach heard her name before he could register it. Immediate convulsions shook his body.

"Whoa, there..." Simon quickly produced a pail from the floor. Ryan grabbed it as his body shook. He'd hardly eaten today and couldn't imagine what would be pumping out of his stomach. Simon offered the wet cloth when he seemed to be finished. Still no mention of the abductions. Or Wade.

"Thank you." He wiped away the mess. "I appreciate all this." This was the second time Simon had used that phrase with him: *like family.* His mind flooded with things he shouldn't say. *I'm holding your daughter against her will! I'm about to take everything away from you! You shouldn't be taking care of me.* He reached for the bottle of water. Maybe it was the irony of the situation, or the pity he felt towards this man, that made him suddenly trust that it was safe to drink.

"You want to tell me what happened tonight, son?"

Ryan looked down from the bottle. Simon was studying him again. "I don't know." It was all he could come up with in the moment. Wade had let him live. Which meant he wasn't done with him. If an alert was put out for his arrest and he was brought in, the cops would hear Wade's ideas regarding Ryan's involvement in the death of James and his parents. That couldn't happen.

"What? I mean, how can you not know? Who did this to you?" Simon leaned forward, shaking his head. "It's okay to tell me, we can get this sorted out together."

Together?

"He must have hit me pretty hard", Ryan offered, lowering the bottle. "I don't remember much."

"But why you? Maybe this has something to do with Annie and Teagan. Someone could be targeting your team."

An interesting idea.

"Hmm", Ryan mused, trying to focus. Simon deepened his stare, as if asking for more. "I mean... that wouldn't be good", Ryan fumbled.

"But he took the chance that you'd remember him and go to the police." Simon furrowed his brow even deeper. "That just doesn't make sense."

Yes, it did. Wade knew Ryan wouldn't go to the police. Besides knowing his past, he'd also threatened to kill innocent people if Ryan didn't cooperate. "Well I don't know, sir." Ryan extended and relaxed his fingers. Blood spattered up his sleeve. Simon must have given him a drug already because his mind was clearing by the minute. As far as he could tell no bones were broken, but his ribs were extremely sore. But that wasn't all he needed to be worried about - Wade knew about his soccer team. Danger surrounded his life and relationships now. The ransom would give him an opportunity to disappear with Annie and Teagan to keep them safe. Then perhaps Wade would leave as well to find him, which would protect the team. He'd pulled off a vanishing act before and it had worked for thirteen years. Even as he thought about it though, guilt turned in his chest like a blade. A pull on his heart for the man sitting in front of him. He would have done anything as a teenager to return even one boy safely to his family. But this situation was different.

Annie was in danger from Simon, after-all.

"Have you ever heard about God?" Simon blurted. The statement startled Ryan. It was forced. Awkward. God? *God?* Simon had a medical mind. He of all people should know that beliefs in unseen powers were crazy! Tangibility was all that mattered. Hard cash, fitness and women. A wave of shock hit him in then - the last moments of consciousness in the barn...

Please...God... help....

His words. His *'prayer'*. The second one today. He'd seen death in Wade's eyes and had known his life was over. Yet here he was, very much alive. In the private home and care of a physician. He blinked. Then blinked again.

Simon saw the confusion and cleared his throat. "I'm sorry. It's a new concept to me. I sound like I'm losing my mind here, don't I?"

"What?" Ryan vaguely heard his comments. "No, sir." He swallowed. "What about Him?"

Lunatic! His mind screamed. *Don't talk, just get yourself out of here!*

"One of the school counsellors told me told about prayer. Said that God hears us." His eyes begged Ryan to agree.

Ryan cleared grogginess from his throat. "I guess I've heard something similar." Way too many times. Coaching Cadence Rhodes for the last two years had come with numerous conversations about her God. *'He helps me through all kinds of things.'* She'd tell him at practise. He pictured her bouncing ponytail and bright eyes, accompanying stories of 'miracles' and her prayer life. Two years of this! If focusing wasn't so hard he would have rolled his eyes at the thought.

"Annie's been going to Cadence's church. I guess I wanted to find out what they were telling her there." Simon explained.

So, that's where she got those crazy ideas. "I see. What do you think about that?"

Simon scratched his head and adjusted his glasses again. "I still don't know too much, but it would be nice to believe that someone is watching over her."

"Yeah…" Reasoning and speculation battled in Ryan's mind. Both his prayers had been answered tonight, and he had no control over either of them. Could it be possible that the God Cadence spoke of really was who she claimed?

"I'll grab some clean blankets for you." This comment jerked his mind back to the room. Blankets?

"Sorry?"

"My wife, Lydia, keeps the blankets in the hall closet. She's asleep upstairs or she'd be right beside me helping you. I'll be right back."

"Wait..." He tried to find meaning to that sentence. "Oh! No, no... I need to get home." He couldn't stay *here*.

"Don't be ridiculous, you're in no shape to be left on your own. I have plenty of space here. You can have some breakfast in the morning and we'll call the police from here." Simon folded his arms over his mock neck sweater and set his jaw as if the conversation was over.

"No, really, you don't have to do this." He started to slide off the bed and stood, hoping his fake enthusiasm would give his body the stamina to walk out of there. His legs shook but he had more feeling in them than when he'd first woken up. "Thank you, sir, but can you take me back to my jeep?"

115

"That seems unnecessary. I can drop you off in the morning after you've had something to eat."

Ryan licked his lips and exhaled slowly. "No. Please, I have a dog who needs attention and I don't sleep well when I'm not in my own bed." Other than him owning a dog, neither of the statements were true. Of course, he did need to check on Jada, but it wasn't an emergency.

"Young man, your heart rate is dangerously low and you have a fever of 105 degrees. If you don't want to stay here that's fine, but I'm not letting you off on your own until you're somewhat stabilized." He dropped his arms after a moment, and reached for the first-aid kit. "This will help with the pain." He grabbed a bottle. "There's enough in here for tonight and the next day or so. And if you need something else in the morning I want you to call me, okay? I can drive you to the hospital then or write you a prescription."

Ryan swallowed and met his eyes. Never in his life had someone insisted on taking care of him. He took the bottle. Naproxen. "Thanks." Accepting hospitality from the man he was helping destroy. Not part of the plan. He looked at the bottle instead of at Simon.

"Let's get some food into you before we go. I insist." He squeezed Ryan's shoulder.

"No, sir, really, I'll be fine by the time we get back to my jeep."

Simon raised his eyebrows with an expression that made Ryan feel as though he were being lectured as a teenager. "When was the last time you ate, son?"

"Supper." He lied.

"What'd you have for supper?"

Any other day a perfectly good meal would have come straight to his mind, but instead he fumbled over several words, and wasn't even sure what he ended up saying.

"Right. I'm not taking no for an answer. Come on." Simon turned and pulled him into the hall, and Ryan followed because he had nowhere else to go. Robbing Simon had made sense when Ryan had been roped into this scheme months ago. The heartless story he'd been told had made him pin Simon as a selfish, wealthy brute. But this father was different than he'd been led to believe.

Chapter 10

8:38 AM

"Are you alone?"

"Excuse me? I haven't heard from you in over twenty-four hours and that's how you address me?" Heat spread up Michelle's neck. She sat alone at the high crystal table in the dining room. Sunlight floated down around her from the skylight windows. She'd almost destroyed her cell when his name appeared on the screen. "Where were you last night? Were you at the bunker? I swear, if you're getting too attached to those girls, I'm going -"

"What? No, Michelle, I...I ran into someone from my past." He paused again.

"And? You better have more than that for an excuse!"

"Well, I - we got into a fight -" He coughed.

"You did what now?" Her fingers pressed against her temples. "Did you get arrested? Are you calling me from jail?"

"No", he growled. "Nobody saw anything." He waited a moment. "Look, I didn't ask for this, okay? He found me and he had a gun. I didn't have a choice."

"A gun?" Her tone softened. "Are you in the hospital? Are you alright?"

"Yeah, I'm fine. I'm at home." She waited for more but he wasn't speaking without prompts.

She sighed. "Well, what did the past want with you?"

"He knows what I did, Elle." His nickname for her.

"Oh." If the police brought him in for questioning he could spill her secrets. "So,   you took care of him?"

"What?"

"You took him out, right?" She glanced at her Rolex watch.

"What? Why would you think that?"

"If you let him live he'll tell someone, Ryan! You can't have baggage from your past bothering you right now!" The line was silent. "Ryan, you didn't answer my question about where you were last night."

"Never mind."

"No, tell me. What did he do?" She massaged the back of her neck. "Where is he now?"

"It's nothing." He coughed a moment later.

"Well, it better be something for you not to return my calls!" Her voice sliced the air. "Hey, answer me!"

"A fist fight", he paused. "I saw a doctor. Got home late and meant to call but I passed out right away." Michelle turned the information over.

"I see. And the other man? You'll take care of it, right?

"Elle, I -"

"Ryan, you can't possibly be thinking we can let him live with what he knows!" She smacked the glass tabletop. "Not now, when we're so close to collecting the ransom!"

"I know that… but I'm not going out looking for another fight."

"That's not what I'm asking you to do." The line went silent again. "Ryan, you're a killer. The sooner you accept that about yourself, the better off you'll be. Tie up your loose ends so we can start our new life together!" She heard his raspy breaths as he considered her words. "Babe, I need you to have your mind here in the present. The past will be there to deal with after we finish this job. And you need to be ready to kill again if I ask you to." She hesitated. "Whether it's an outsider or your bratty hostages."

"That wasn't the deal! You said they were just pawns for your brother's revenge." She heard him cough again and try to cover a groan.

"What's the matter?" He didn't respond. She sighed, "There's nothing to worry about. The money comes in and everyone lives." Her words lingered. He wasn't arguing. "I assume the plans for picking up the ransom are ready?"

"Yeah. It'll be simple." He was silent a minute. "I'm a good person, Elle."

"Of course, babe. You're the most noble man I know. I wouldn't have you any other way." She tousled her hair, and glanced at her nails. One had chipped.

"Well. I'm not a killer. I'm a survivor."

"Yes, you're right. I'm sorry, babe. I shouldn't have said that." She flipped to the next page in the Designer's catalogue in front of her and hung up.

What a poor boy. Trying so hard to be a man. His youthful edge was amusing and he'd be fun to keep around for awhile. If he cooperated. She didn't want to kill him. But his aggressive stubbornness would tip her hand if he didn't let up soon. She yawned and dialed the spa to set up a manicure.

***

Ryan hung up. His jaw ached from speaking. *Yes, he was a survivor.* One who had to kill to stay alive. The triple homicide had been necessary. And yes, he'd considered ending Wade too. Could he have done it if Wade hadn't overpowered him? Maybe. But death was a dark place to create and if he had the choice he'd never go there again.

His ribs throbbed and his head pounded. He tossed the phone onto the nightstand and slipped his bare legs out from beneath the thin blanket. It was soaked like usually from the sweat that accompanied his nightmares. Occasionally he could go two or three nights before changing the sheets. He ran his fingers back and forth through his short, brown hair then slowly swung his feet off the bed. The cool, hardwood floor calmed the heat coursing through his body. Arguments with Michelle often managed to rub him the wrong way and send him into self-loathing. Luckily today his physical pain demanded all his attention. He pushed away from the bed and stood. His legs still shook under his weight. He braced against the olive colored wall and moved forward. Each step irritated a different muscle and he made a different sound for each stab of pain. He swallowed hard and stopped moving. He turned his torso and leaned on the wall for support. Hot white stars swam in his vision. He breathed deeply and looked to his night table for water. A half-filled glass sat next to his black digital clock. He couldn't reach it from where he stood though. His burning throat begged him to go back for it, to cool the migraine and tension. No. He was halfway to the bedroom door already and shower would be better than a simple drink.

Priorities. They had guided his existence. Never take a step back if you don't need to.

His gaze lingered on the water another second, then he turned towards the door. Focus. A few more steps. He wanted to rush forward, to dare his body to challenge the pain. But even as he considered it, his disciplined patience ordered him to move with care. He exhaled slowly and leaned back against the wall. His muscles needed to move so they could unkink and heal. He leaned forward into a deep stretch.

"Gah!" He gasped. Stabbing pain shot down his legs. He squeezed his eyes shut as his muscles burned from the movement. He clenched his teeth. Barking and thudded paws barreled down the hall towards his closed bedroom door. He straightened up slowly. "It's okay, Jada. It's alright. Go lie down." She let out a concerned whine but then dropped beside the door. He stretched over both legs individually, then moved slowly through his hamstrings, soleus, and Achilles. It helped. He straightened and tipped his neck to each side then rolled his shoulders several times. The next steps he took were easier as his body began to wake up. He massaged the back of his neck and palmed the door knob. Immediately he heard Jada jump back up, then groan through a stretch. Ryan took a breath and opened the door. Jada bunted his legs wildly with her head, and pushed between them. Her tail repeatedly whacked the wall and her bright blue eyes darted over his features. He lowered and massaged the fur behind her ears. She pushed into his touch.

"Such a good girl." He managed to kiss her above the eyes before she insisted on licking his face with her rough tongue. The contact over his bruises and scraps hurt but he allowed it, because it cooled the heat from his headache. He kissed her again then stood and ambled towards the bathroom. He stretched one arm across his chest as he walked in. The bathroom tiles were even colder than the hardwood floor in his room. Small chills shot up his legs and his mind woke up a bit more. He stopped in front of the mirror.

Ouch. He looked like a corpse. His face had taken on various shades of purple, brown and gray. One eye was still swollen completely shut.

Damn, Spencer.

He grabbed the cup he kept on the sink and filled it twice, inhaling the contents in seconds. His dry, burning throat both loved and hated him for drinking so fast. The naproxen was behind the mirror with his toothbrush. He tossed back a pill and grabbed toothpaste. Opening his mouth wide enough to clean it hurt like hell. But he tried to gently clean his bottom gums anyway. He spit into the sink but a heavy string of drool came out instead.

"Come on..." He growled. Spitting again, which added to the frustration. Finally, he turned on the tap and lowered his face as close to the pouring faucet as his neck and back could handle. The cold water ran over his hands first. He lingered in the refreshing moment, then splashed his face. The heat beneath the bruising faded a little. He repeated the action. Then again. And again. His saliva disappeared as water splashed over his skin and started rejuvenating his body. Water dripped down his neck onto his bare chest. He flinched at the shiver but also appreciated it. After a few moments, he rested his hands on the sink and let droplets fall off his hair and skin. He breathed deeply, bidding the coolness to spread through his body.

He pulled the mirror back and grabbed mouthwash. The muscles in his mouth cooperated more now and he swished slowly, then spit. No extra saliva this time. Goosebumps crawled up his skin, which was good. A normal reaction to the cool temperature in his home. He pushed away from the sink for a shower. The steam drifted out of stall inviting him in. Once inside, the heat did wonders for his stiff muscles. Crisp scents of mountain air body wash clung to his clean skin and hair. He usually didn't linger, but today he stood facing the streaming water, letting the relaxing sensation envelope him. After fifteen minutes he stepped out onto a shaggy brown mat, snagging a white towel and flipping it around his waist. He raked his fingers through his wet hair, spraying water beads onto his sun-tanned shoulders. He leaned close to the mirror to consider removing his morning stubble. But a razor still seemed like a terrible idea. He grunted and pulled away.

He valued appearance. Call him a control freak, but presentation played a big role in survival. He ambled back to his room and pulled on sweats, then meandered through the kitchen, and grabbed a water bottle and an apple. He finally settled himself on the living room floor and began to stretch. Now that he could think more clearly, he started to re-play the previous day's events in his mind. Being confronted with his past at the gym and the beating from Wade which reminded him of so many fights with his father. And realizing no matter how strong he had become he was still just as helpless in the ropes as he had been as a youth.

Then there was Simon's rescue after Ryan had been left on the street. Instead of being picked up by a cop or by someone else who would do him more harm, he'd been found by a doctor. And cared for in a quiet, clean home instead of a dirty hospital where nurses would fuss over him. Ryan hated sympathy and his close contacts knew that. But Simon's actions had been different. Respectful and genuine. No one had treated him like that in all the years he could remember.

After he'd dropped him off at his jeep, Simon insisted that he go to emergency in the morning for x-rays of his ribs and to get checked for a concussion. It was a kind suggestion but unnecessary. Ryan may not have a Doctorate like Simon, but he'd focused his entire life around the around muscle development, including injuries and recovery. It was his specialty. He probably knew more about it than Simon did. Enough to look after himself anyway. He contemplated now if he could make it out to the bunker in his condition. He was still dizzy and his muscles ached, but now that he was thinking about, some cardio would help loosen him up. He'd spend an hour or so here on the floor stretching, cancel his gym clients, and take his time getting started with the day. Then he'd buy something nice for the girls to eat today. A small way to pay Simon back. He whistled for Jada.

"Good girl." Jada bounded over from where she'd been wrestling with a toy. "Phone." Ryan made a rectangle with his hands, using his thumbs and pointer fingers to form L's. She took off to find it and moments later came crashing into the living room with the protected phone case in her mouth. "Good girl!" He made a big deal of praising her and rubbing her down before checking the weather. A cool morning. He'd wear a thicker sweater than usual to keep his core warm and prevent shock. And today would be a bike day. Running probably wasn't a good option yet.

J. M. Bergman

***

Annie woke to slow thuds coming from outside her room. She blinked at the darkness. The large windows above her bed should at least be spilling light from the street lights. And fresh air usually came in through the open screen. But stale oxygen hung around her instead. Light slipped under the door and a dog barked. But she didn't own a dog. She tried to move her hands just as she had almost every time she'd woken up over the previous days. But they were bound together behind her back.

Right. Bound as a hostage.

Waking up each day forgetting about her dark circumstances brought hope for a few seconds at least. A small time where she still lived as a sophomore in a safe neighborhood and thrived on the soccer field. But the reality of her circumstance always sunk into her chest soon after. Irrevocable and sharp. Coach said that - *No. No, Annie,* she reprimanded. The lessons from 'Coach' about staying strong through hard times were lies.

Worse than lies.

She'd been conned. Betrayed.

And now she sat in the darkness, bandaged and cold, in darkness. A tear slipped down her cheek. A few moments of silence passed. Then his shadow blotted out the light beneath the door, and she heard him turn the key. Her pulse quickened and the door creaked open with a squeal of rust. She squinted and ducked her head to the side, away from the lifeless light. After a few seconds, she looked back and saw that he was braced against the doorframe. His silhouette looked bulky which meant he probably wore layers today. The thought made her angry. He knew the temperature had dropped but only cared about himself. His body cast a long shadow over her.

"Hey, ladies." He coughed into his sleeve. "Aaagh", he groaned quietly and lowered to his haunches. One hand braced against the ground while the other massaged his side. Maybe he had a cramp. Serves him right. Oh, how she hoped at least had a cramp. He coughed again, then half-crawled the short distance to sit in front of them and sat down cross-legged. He slowly removed his bag. "You two awake?"

She ducked her head down again. A sob still choked her throat and she desperately hoped it would go away before she was expected to talk. She hated showing emotion to him. Almost as much as she hated his existence.

Breathe in; breathe out, she coached herself. Again. The steady breaths might signal her to be asleep - but then he would try and wake her. She realized her mistake and sucked in the last breath, but it was too late.

"Hey." He wiggled her shoe. "Wake up." She opened her eyes and saw his other arm extended toward Teagan. His posture appeared laid back. Different from last time when he woke them up with cold water in the face. She grunted so he'd stopped touching her once he

128

knew she was up. Teagan made some soft noises too. Ryan settled back on the floor and began pulling items out of the bag. She couldn't see the knife and his other tools of captivity, but she knew they'd appear soon so he could make their lives more miserable. "I brought strawberries and yogurt. You ladies like that, right?"

Wait… *Strawberries?* Annie blinked several times, as if the motion would give his statement more meaning. Strawberries signified sweet summer fantasies and picnics by the lake. Innocence and laughter. That couldn't have been what he said. And if he did say it, he must have meant something else. His cruel nature couldn't possibly have crossed with such a lovely thing. Unless he said it to spite them. To get their hopes up. She let her eyebrows fall at the thought. He'd probably shine a light in her face any minute to see if she'd fallen for his ploy.

He coughed again, then cleared his throat. He rolled his shoulders and she heard him sigh as he cracked his neck on both sides. "Alright, I'll make you a deal: you ladies promise me you won't misbehave and I'll let you eat together in here today."

Together? Annie tried to clear her mind. She couldn't have heard him right.

"Well?"

She glanced at Teagan and saw confusion on her face too. She turned back and nodded with a shrug.

"What about you, Teagan?" He didn't sound angry, but his voice was lower than usual. She cleared her throat and gave a muffled 'yes'. "Okay, great." He reached for Annie's face and worked the edge of the tape at her mouth, and a small piece on the corner peeled away. "Ready?"

He'd never asked before. "Mmhmm?"

Yank! One quick motion and it was off. She gasped and whimpered, without meaning to, and clenched her teeth together to stop the tears. The skin around her lips felt as though a hundred tiny ants had attacked. If it weren't so cold down here, it probably wouldn't hurt as much as it did.

"Sorry." He muttered.

Sorry? You're sorry?

"You'll be okay." He slid sideways to reach for the tape on Teagan's face. His shadow moved too, and for a moment the light landed on a large carton of berries, a few cups of yogurt, and water bottles. He'd been telling the truth. "Okay, Teagan, ready?"

Screech!

"Ahh!" She gasped and dropped her head. "Do you even realize how much it hurts every time you do that? Maybe one day someone will duct tape your mouth shut. We'll see how much you like it then!"

Ryan scrunched both pieces of tape in his hand and dropped them into his bag. No smart remarks or authoritarian statements. He pulled out the knife and Annie felt every muscle in her body tighten. *Breathe through it.* That's all she could do. He would do whatever he wanted to regardless of her consent. *Focus on the berries.* She took another breath. She glanced up and saw his shadowed figure watching

130

her. She took another jagged breath, just reached for her arm. She flinched.

"Hey -!" He drew back. "Annie..."

"Sorry", she whispered. She should have said it louder. He let the moment pass, then pulled her forward by the toes of her shoes. "I'm going to cut your hands free. No smart moves from you, got it?" He turned and coughed to the side again.

"Okay." Louder than before. He took her arm and turned her away from him to reach her wrists.

"Have at it." He scrunched the tape in his hand and pulled Teagan forward to do the same thing. Annie reached for a yogurt cup and spoon. She gingerly lifted the container and peeled back the plastic. Creamy goodness.

"Here, you ladies help yourselves to these." He opened the berries and set the carton between them, then moved the water bottles within arm's reach.

"You must've woken up in a good mood this morning." Teagan quipped as she grabbed a yogurt. She ripped it open and licked the back of the plastic. He watched them eat for a moment, then took a water for himself. They sat quietly for about fifteen minutes. He let Teagan use the washroom and told her she could shower if she wanted to, which she did. He sat guard in the doorway while Teagan was in the washroom. Annie watched him curiously. He sat with his knees up and arms draped over top. Jada whined from the other room. He turned to Jada and that's when she saw the marks on his face. He'd been injured.

She cleared her throat, working up the nerve to ask about it. He glanced back into the room.

"Are you alright?" She settled on softly.

"I'm fine." He coughed again and adjusted his hat.

Well, you don't look 'fine'! She wanted to spit the remark back at him. He'd brought delicious food today, but that didn't clear his slate. Not in her books. He could at least talk with her instead of sitting here in silence. A few minutes later Teagan walked out, carrying with her the fresh smell of clean hair. She sat back down and massaged the back of Annie's neck while Ryan slid across the floor on the seat of his pants.

"Ryan?"

"What?" He looked at Teagan before rolling out a new piece of tape.

"Can we have another blanket? It's colder in here now."

He ripped the tape with his teeth. "Sure."

Really? No arguing?

"Oh...thanks, Ryan." She said after the initial surprise. He covered her mouth with tape.

"Okay, Annie: washroom, shower, and back out here in fifteen." He freed her ankles and pushed himself back to the door with his hands. Annie went straight for the shower, where hot water pulled out her chills. Hopefully her body could keep the heat in until he brought another blanket. She finished up and walked back to the wall.

"Thanks for the showers", she said as Ryan slid up in front of her. He made a sound as if to speak, but gagged instead. He covered his

132

mouth and gagged again. Annie saw his whole body shudder. Teagan elbowed her and she raised an eyebrow in return. Had something upset her? They couldn't talk about it, so she moved over to make space between them, in case Teagan was thinking Ryan might throw up on one of them. He sat still, with his hand at his mouth. He'd stopped shaking. Annie had never seen him in pain before...it was interesting to watch. She wished the moment would last forever. Teagan screamed from behind the duct tape. They both looked up at her. She bulged her eyes, then squeezed them shut with another shriek.

"Hey, what -" Ryan started. Teagan bounced her heels on the cement with another scream. "Teagan, stop -" He reached forward and ripped off the tape and she kept screaming. "Hey!" Jada bounded into the room and barrelled over Teagan's legs, yelping with concern. She bunted her head against Teagan's face and she sniffed her entire body furiously. Ryan shouted over her shrieks. "Stop! Use your words."

"In my eye!" She cried and screamed again. "My eye!" Jada continued to inspect Teagan's whole body.

"Jada, no! Get -" He gasped as Jada turned and started to sniff his face and whimper. "Come on!" He tried to push her away. "Jada, sit! Jada!" She pushed into him and slobbered his face. "No! No, girl, not now!" He did what he could to block his face. Finally, at her own whim, she backed away and sat beside Teagan, panting. Ryan let out a labored breath. He grabbed a flashlight from his bag. "Okay, Teagan, let me look."

She wailed and choked on her sobs as he leaned in "Hey, easy, take a breath…" He shone the light on her squinting eyes. "Okay, which one?"

"My right eye!"

"Okay…" He reached in with two fingers and pried it open. She smashed her forehead down onto his face and Annie heard a crack. "AH!" He hollered, ripping back.

"Run!" Teagan screamed. Annie had realized her intentions when Ryan's nose broke and she was already out the door.

J. M. Bergman

Chapter 11

Annie tore towards the looming staircase. Numbing fear sapped her stamina and she tripped on the second stair, smashing her knee on the next one. She fumbled and caught her balance as she took the next few stairs in a daze. Jada barked and plowed past her to the top, nearly knocking off the staircase in the process. Annie raced forward one step at a time. Almost there. Her foot abruptly anchored in place, and she fell over the next few stairs. She gasped and looked down. Ryan's bloody hand reached through the suspended staircase and held her ankle. He clutched his sweater to the gushing wound on his face with his other hand. He was hunched forward and blood was spattered across his temples. Puffy, purple and brown skin surrounded one eye slit. His lifted sweater pulled away from his skin and she saw dark bruising on his ribs.

She yanked at her foot but his grip tightened.

"What's your plan, Annie?" He asked in a shaky, muffled voice. She held tightly to the railing and desperately pulled at her ankle. But his fingers wrapped tighter.

"Help!" She screamed at the flat door above. "Somebody help me!" Jada nervously tried to spin on the steps above her. "He-lllllp!" She screamed again, drawing out the word. She let her eyes dart around the strange room and met Ryan's unconcerned, ghostly stare.

"What was your plan?" He repeated stiffly from behind the cloth and blood.

"To get away from you!" She screamed down. Twisted emotions that she held onto for too long erupted from inside her like a cannon. "You're a liar and a fake!"

He didn't blink. Or flinch.

"I hope you choke on that blood and die in your sleep!" An image so violent had never crossed her mind. His glare didn't change. She looked back up, grasped both sides of the railing and screamed while she yanked at his grasp. Jada howled with her screams and jumped on her front paws.

"This can go two ways, Annie." He spoke with a dangerous tone. She continued to yank at her ankle. "You come down now: we'll figure this out. But if you go outside, through that door, there's no turning back. I will catch you."

Mind games. He'd said that himself once. "Let me go!" He lowered his eyebrows, but they shot up in the next instant as his body snapped forward in convulsions. His grip loosened and she slammed
137

her other foot down onto his wrist repeatedly. He hollered and fell away. She scrambled forward and managed to jimmy her way around Jada.

Two more stairs!

She grabbed the latch and pushed. It was cold and the weight didn't budge. She pushed harder and it slowly lifted up and away, creaking as it went. Crisp, fresh air and blinding light swallowed her whole. She gasped and squinted, stumbled, then started to run forward blindly. Her legs buckled and she face-planted into the hard ground. Groping at the grass, she struggled to her knees and then up, panting. Deep green pines and dark cedars surrounded her. She careened forward and spun. Thick brush extended on all sides and a light blue sky peeked down through overhead branches. Flattened, yellowing grass gave the faintest hint of a path. With no other choice, she tore ahead into green and brown shadows.

***

Ryan collapsed and hit the floor, spewing vomit and saliva from his mouth. The contents splashed up from the cement and his body shook. The stinging in his wrist shot pain up his arm, but he forced himself to ignore it as he held himself up with his hands against the floor. After a few minutes, thin strings of saliva, mixed with dripping blood from his nose, hung from his face. He heard Jada bound down the stairs.

"Jada, stop!" He ordered, with more authority than before. Now at the base of the stairs she spun nervously and took a step towards him. "No!" He pointed to the other side of the room. She howled and hopped on her paws. "Back. Get -" He coughed and threw up again. He dropped his hand just in time to support his body from falling forward. Tension, stress and anger spewed out with incredible force. A wave of hot and cold ran through him, then finally it ended. He could feel his energy start to come back and his muscles began to reawaken, charging him to take back control of the situation. He ripped the sweater over his head and tossed it. His sweaty black t-shirt stuck to his skin. He grabbed his nose with both hands and, in one movement, reset it. "Gah!" He closed his eyes and pressed his fists into his quads, waiting for his body to calm.

He took another slow breath, then glared ahead to where Teagan cringed against the wall. The light illuminated her paling face. He could see the fear in her eyes from here.

Yeah, you better be scared...

He pushed up and snatched the sweater off the ground in one movement, then wiped his face with it. He stormed into the cell and straight to the washroom. "Jada!" He snapped his fingers, and she followed. He splashed water up to his face and grabbed a towel. Then pushed away and headed to the wall where Teagan sat, quivering.

"Wait - no, no, wait Ryan, sorry, I'm sorry!" She ducked away and screamed as he stopped in front of her. He lowered to a crouch and waited for her to open her eyes.

"You've pushed my hand, Fischer. And you're gonna be sorry." She sucked her lips in below her glassy eyes.

Good. Now sit here and think about all the terrible things I could do to you.

"I'll deal with you when I get back." What he really wanted to do was beat her senseless now. Maybe break her nose and a few other small bones. But his thoughts rebuked him. Letting negative emotions drive his actions had rarely paid off. He stood, grabbed Annie's blanket, and left Teagan shivering in the darkness. Then he and Jada shot up the stairs.

***

Annie tripped forward. Thick forest grew tall around her and the path had disappeared about a hundred metres back, but she didn't dare turn around to find it again. She shot a glance over her shoulder. Still no sign of him.

Panic spilled out her mouth with each breath. Ryan's distorted face flashed across her mind.

'If you go through that door, there's no turning back. I will catch you.'

She ran as if those words didn't pull her back. As if she believed she could outrun him.

Her dirty clothes stuck to her sweaty skin. She ducked to avoid a hanging branch with dead leaves, but she ended up hitting it with the top of her head, and it snapped. A black bird suddenly dove within inches of her face. She screamed and shot her hands up, but kept running.

How had this happened? Breakfast and a shower. A calm morning. Then without warning events had spiraled out of control. Teagan's attack. Her escape. Ryan's bloody face. Then there were the words she'd screamed at Ryan as he held onto her ankle.

'I hope you choke on your blood and die in your sleep!'

Disrespect on the field came at a high price, and she'd cringed at Teagan's punishments before, but Teagan had never said something like *that* to Ryan.

If he caught up with her, he'd probably kill her.

When he caught up with her.

No! She tried to silence the thought and convince herself that she could get away. It had to be possible. How far could they be from a highway? Dodge a tree trunk, side step a bush, duck under low branches. She could do this.

She saw a clearing ahead and sprinted faster through the dry grass and leaves. If she could make it out into the open, she'd be able to cover ground more quickly. *Bam!* Her foot caught in something below and she fell forwards, landing on a dead tree trunk.

She managed to hold back her scream as tears spilled down her cheeks. It took a moment for her to catch her breath before she pulled her bloody knee away. Blood soaked into her jeans around the gash. But she had to keep moving.

She looked back and spun around in case he attacked from the side. Still nothing. She staggered up, ignoring the pain. Then turned and pushed forward in what she hoped was the direction she'd been heading.

***

Ryan rolled the blanket into a small ball and held it to Jada's nose.

"Let's find her, girl", he ruffled the fur behind her ears. She tore off into the woods. He tightened his jaw and sprinted after her. Annie had found his trail. Impressive. She had about a ten minute head start. And she was fast. But he knew these woods well, and if she'd wandered from the path in any direction, the thick growth would slow her down.

Admittedly, closing a large distance between them would give him time to cool off, which was a good thing. He hadn't decided yet what to do with her when he found her, but at least a dozen scenarios had run through his mind since he left the bunker.

He'd regret all of them. And only a few ended without her blood on his hands.

Jada darted in and out of sight through trees and around bushes. Typical of their daily runs. Early afternoon sunlight flickered through the forest canopy overhead. The temperature had risen and his body heat quickly increased too and he appreciated having left the sweater behind. His runners pounded the dirt and twigs below. Greens, browns and grays whipped past his agile body, and fresh vitality raced through his blood. The same ambition he threw into disciplined, rigorous training now boiled beneath his skin. Throw that together with the previous night's events, a broken nose and a lippy hostage, and you got a dangerous man.

A dangerous, angry man.

A small part of him hoped she'd get away. For her sake. Then her dramatic antics and emotions wouldn't be his problem anymore. But if he allowed that, she'd fall prey to Michelle. Which wouldn't be so bad. It would come with a pricey reward too, since Michelle wanted her dead anyway. And he could almost guarantee that her death would be painful. He slowed to a jog. What did he hope to gain by protecting either her or Teagan?

A few days ago, it had seemed to be the right thing to do, given what he knew. And helping them was a small form of redemption for all the lives he couldn't save in his past. But no one involved appreciated his work. And Annie and Teagan had a long way to go before they would thank him for anything.

An image of his soccer team flashed in his memory. Their hard training and laughing faces. He pictured Annie running onto the field after high-fiving him with a smile. Teagan tearing up the offense, dribbling down the green. Their curious ideas about life and the small accomplishments they shared with him. He shook his head once and whistled for Jada. A few seconds later she broke through the trees and tore back. He crouched and held out the blanket for her to sniff again.

He had no idea what kind of future awaited them. But no one was getting murdered on his watch. Annie would pay for her disrespect though.

***

A branch with green and yellow leaves slapped Annie's face. She gasped and squinted through the sting. A sharp cramp tore at her sides and each inhale hurt a little more than the last. A huge tree trunk lay fallen ahead and she considered dodging it but found herself crawling over before the thought sank in. She pulled herself up and over and her knees buckled as she landed. She fell forward and landed on the cool, dirt floor with a grunt. She dug her fingers into the soil and tried to catch her breath.

But then she heard fast footsteps approaching from behind. *No!* She pushed up off her hands and staggered forward into a jog. She wasn't even sure how much longer she could keep going, and in her mind, she began to accept that her end was near.

This is your only chance!

Would he kill her quickly or draw it out?

No! You have to get away!

He'd make it slow, and take time to remind her how she'd messed up... and how he was disappointed in her. Make her do push ups first.

You're giving up! You can't let him win!

*Okay, time to think outside of the box...*He's impossible to outrun, but maybe she could hide somewhere, or change directions and double back.

He's sick and injured... so maybe she could hit him with a stick or a rock and finish him off. About twenty feet ahead the trees thinned into another green clearing. She needed to get across. Her lungs felt like they'd explode as she pushed herself forward.

Footsteps pounded up behind her! She screamed just as Jada shot past and skidded as she turned and ran back towards her. Annie stumbled to a stop and threw her hands out in defense. Jada ran into her legs, licked her hand then stretched and bunted against her legs again. Annie sighed in relief and wiped her sweaty hands on her shirt. Maybe the dog had gotten away from Ryan. But then she heard heavier footsteps coming. She gasped and twisted, as she started to run. Then screamed again. Not ten feet away, Ryan sprinted forward, hat backwards above his red face. She twisted forward and ran, and glanced back just before he grabbed her waist and they went down.

***

He hit the ground and leapt to his knees. She screamed again and wrestled free for a split second. But he grabbed her arm and pinned her face down in the dirt. Her long hair tangled fell over her tank top.

"Ryan, please! No... no! I'm so -" She begged, still trying to squirm free. He grabbed her other swinging arm and pulled both wrists up and she screamed. "Ahh! Plea - please -"

"Hey! Shut your mouth!" He pulled her wrists upward a bit harder...she let out a guttural cry, then choked on a sob.

Not so tough now, hey punk?

"I'm sor-ry..." Her voice cracked. He could break her arms. Maybe just one. Jada barked and hopped back and forth beside them.

"Back!" He shouted. Annie arched her torso awkwardly beneath him. "What now, you little brat?" He wiped his forehead on his sleeve and lifted her wrists higher. Another wordless screech. Not much farther to go until - *No.* He couldn't break her bones. Wouldn't. Even though he wanted to. He held on a moment longer then let go. Her hands smacked against the ground. She gasped for air and pulled her shaking fingers through the dirt. A little moan left her lips. "Get up." He lifted his knee and pushed up to his feet. Wrapped bandaging hung from her arms and dragged through the dirt, and the circular Aztec scars on her arms were covered with dirt and sweat. "I said, get up!"

She lifted her chin and stared up at him. Her quivering lips parted and shut repeatedly. Tears pooled at the bottom of her brown eyes. Scared, sad eyes. *Don't you dare think I'll fall for that look.*

146

Though for a heartbeat he couldn't imagine bringing her harm. He swept dirt off his shirt and frowned. She dragged her hands along the ground and slid them beneath her. She looked at him again.

"I..." The edges of her eyes crinkled. "I can't..."

"Oh, no, Missy, you started this fight, now get up and take what's coming to you." She started to whimper and he shook his head, then hoisted her up by the arm. She swayed to find footing and hung in his grasp. Her free hand reached for him, then fell. She tried again. "Stand up, kid."

"I - I'm trying..." She swung for him again, this time grabbing on and gingerly clinging to his forearm. Eventually her hold strengthened into a clutch. He ground his teeth together as he waited and watched the top of her downturned head. He wanted to rip his arm away and let her drop. But then she might stay down and refuse to meet his aggression. And he wasn't finished. Inch by inch her body straightened and her grasp became tighter. After about a minute she let go and stumbled backwards.

"Got any other trash talk you wanna get out before I kick your ass?"

Her eyes widened and beads of sweat shone off her face. She shook her head fast. "Oh, no, no, Ryan, I -"

"Spit it out!"

She paled. "Please, Ryan, I -"

"You what, Annie? Thought you'd break my wrist and get away?" She looked up as her mouth opened and closed, trying to form

147

silent words. He held out his red, swelling wrist and rotated it. "Not today, kid."

"No, no -" Her pupils dilated as he walked against, pushing her backwards. "No, please -" She gasped and held her hands out to stop him. "I'm sorry!" He punched her in the shoulder. Not hard. But enough for a reaction. "Ryan!"

"You need to block!" He walked faster and she tripped backwards. "If you want to fight with me, you have to do better than that!" She stuttered over another string of words and tried to push him back. He punched again and she tried to block with both hands, but he got her in the gut, then flicked her collarbone with his other hand. "Don't leave yourself open!" He backed her into a tree trunk and she flattened her hands against the rough bark. She screamed and kicked at him to shield herself from his next hit. He punched her exposed shoulder twice to make a point. "Block!" She flinched again and swung at his arm. He let her make the hit and push him back a bit. She backed up against the trunk again and held her hands out as shields.

"Ryan, please, I – I wasn't thinking … I won't do -"

"Come on, away from the tree." He stepped back to give her the option to move away. "The bark is rough, it'll hurt more if you push yourself against it like that." He held his palms up to show a moment of truce. She studied him, then did as he said. He punched her in the gut right away, and she winced and cried out, then tried to swat him with both hands, but he hit her unguarded side. Then tapped the side of her head with an open palm. "You just gonna take it, or what?" She ducked and scowled. He tapped the other side of her head.

"Ryan!"

"What?" Hit to her ribs. She tried to catch his fist again and her mouth hung as her eyes darted after his movements. "You got something to say, or not?" He kicked the side of her leg as if dribbling a ball.

"I don't know how to fight!"

"Well, it sure sounded like you were calling me on back in the -" She made a jab for his side and he took the hit, even though the attack was written all over her face. "Okay, what else you got?"

"Ryan, I can't -"

"What else?" Jada howled and shot between them. "Jada! Back! Fight back, Annie, or take the beating!" He punched between her shoulder and collarbone, harder than before. She stumbled backwards, but brought her fists up, balled. She aimed for his chest, but he caught the blow in his palm. "Again!" One fist went low. He caught it. "Again." She swung for his ribs, then his chest again, but he caught the blow. "Again! Faster!" She swung her arms and the sweaty bandages flew. He blocked and punched her in the side. "I can read your moves! Show me more control!" She struck again. Then again. Her long, dirty hair flung through the air with each throw. She punched twice, and at the last second he saw her knee come up for his groin. He twisted his hips and took the hit in the leg. He kicked her feet out from beneath her and she crashed to the ground with a cry. "Cheap shot for cheap shot",

149

he warned. He balled his fists and circled above her. "Get up!" He noticed her bloody knee then. She scrambled backwards, away from him. Dead leaves clung to her jeans. He tilted his head, trying to decide if she had any fight left in her. "I was in your house last night."

"What?" She stopped moving.

"With your dad."

Her expression changed, but he couldn't pinpoint what he saw.

"He made me coffee in your favorite light blue mug. The one your mom liked." *Second cheap shot.* He saw the comment cut her deep and regretted it.

"Stay away from him!" She bared her teeth.

Awesome.

She pushed off the ground. The fight he'd seen in her at the bunker was back. She hesitated, then came at him. She brought her arms up and jabbed, stepping into him as he had done at first. She hit his side, below his ribs, with her small fist, then punched again, then a shot to his collar, which he didn't expect. He deflected it, but she made a satisfying blow to his gut. He staggered for her benefit.

"Good. Now more -"

She punched his ribs hard. His bruised ribs. He snarled and smacked her arm away. But she was already kicking his shin, then his other shin. Then again. Harder. She was growling through her bared teeth. He backpedaled and grabbed her arms to stop her. She tried to yank back. A second passed, then he let her go. She jabbed at his chest and he blocked, but didn't catch the low punch to his gut. He grunted,

150

both annoyed and impressed. He stepped back again, but she kept swinging. Then tried to hook his leg. "Nice try." He swung at her shoulder, but she ducked and sent an excruciating stab up into his under arm. "Hey!" He grabbed her arm and spun her, pinning it against her back again.

"That's not fair!" She kicked back hard into his shin.

"Gah! You're a dirty fighter!" He grabbed her other swinging arm and spread his legs to prevent another direct kick.

"I just watch you and repeat what I see!" She snarled. He ripped her around and stared down at her. She glared back with intensity in her eyes. He pointed two fingers at her.

"You're the erratic one..." Not many would cross him twice like that and have the guts to stare him in the face afterward. "I see it now... you hide behind your 'good girl' facade, but underneath you're a raging ball of aggression!" He traced his mouth with his fingers and placed his hand on his hip. "What are you thinking here, kid?" He could end her. And she knew it.

"I don't care what you do to me anymore! Cadence's God sees everything."

"Oh! You want to bring *God* into this?" He shot back. "I don't see him rescuing you." He searched their surroundings mockingly. Her comment unnerved him though, because he hadn't forgotten his prayer that landed him at Simon's house.

"He's bigger than you!" Her bold eyes dared him to react. He ground his teeth together for a moment, contemplating how to continue.

Yes, she had fight inside her but it would get her into trouble. However he knew firsthand that a fighting spirit could keep a person alive; but she had a lot of learning to do. A mild respect replaced some of his anger.

"Look: you're a tough kid, and I respect that. But you have to choose the right kind of fights to start." He paused and pointed at himself. "I will always win. And unless you want to end up on the ground again today, you need to back down. Now." She glared back and pulled one arm over her chest. "I'm serious, Annie. Let's call this quits, alright?" She studied him a moment longer, then sighed and dropped her shoulders.

"Alright." He cracked his neck. He could come clean with her today. Explain the complicated situation. Prevent any future escape plans. But at what cost? If she knew the truth - the truth about what her dad had done - her fervor would die. "You don't know it yet but I'm the good guy here."

"What are you talking about?" She snapped, sweeping hair away from her dirt stained face.

"Hey - watch your tone."

She narrowed her eyes. Abrasive. He waited. "Sorry."

He nodded. "That's all you get to know for now." He shifted his weight and pointed at her again. "What you did today can't happen again. Do you understand?"

She frowned and sucked in her lips.

"Do you understand?"

"No, I don't understand!" She sliced the air with her hand. "What's going on, Ryan? Why are we out here?" She gestured to the surrounding forest. He returned the frown, then walked past her to grab his hat from where it had fallen. "We don't deserve to be locked up or abused like this! Why won't you tell me?"

"You stepped way out of line today, Annie." He positioned his hat facing forward, then turned back to look at her. "In the real world, outside of school, you can't degrade someone the way you did and expect to get anything from them." He moved around her to pick up the blanket he'd used to find her. "Life doesn't work like that." He glanced over his shoulder and saw her face flush and twist with what looked like disappointment. Maybe shame.

"But Ryan..."

He looked up and waited for her to go on.

"You tied us up and locked us underground!" She dropped her open palms. "Doesn't it make sense that we would try and escape?"

"Not the right answer." He shook his head and dropped his gaze. One end of the cloth sat in each hand. He began flipping it over itself to create a rope of sorts, and tied it around his waist so it'd be easy to carry back.

"No, I mean, I shouldn't have said what I did -" She stumbled. "I wasn't thinking straight. I'm sorry -"

He met her eyes again.

"I'm sorry", she repeated. He walked towards her.

"So, you don't hope I '*choke on my blood and die in my sleep*'?"
He mocked. Deep red burned across her face. She opened her mouth,
but then pressed her lips together. He grabbed one wrist, then took her
other hand and tied them together in front of her. "It's okay." He said
as he finished. "Listen, your anger can keep you moving. But you need
more control. More focus. Got it?" He watched her lips fall into a sulk,
but then she nodded. "Okay. Let's get back. Walk in front of me, I'll
tell you where to go." He grabbed her arm as she turned away. "And if
you try anything stupid on the way back, you'll be doing push-ups until
you pass out. Got it?" She crossed her arms, and for a moment he felt
as though he was trying to reason with Teagan. "Got it?" He raised his
eyebrows.

"Maybe I'm not going to let you boss me around anymore."
He took a threatening step closer. "Try me."
She scowled and turned away.

***

Annie walked carefully through the tall grass. A small critter
scurried up a dying tree and a frightened bird took flight. Ryan had tied
the bandages over her knee and now he walked closely behind her. She
had no idea where she was going and thought it made more sense that
he would lead, but he said he wanted her to watch her step not his back.
And her hands could break a fall if she tripped again.

Somewhere back when Ryan was yelling at her, when she thought she'd die, it had clicked. Nobody could protect her now. No one knew where she was. Except Cadence's God. And that's when she'd decided she believed. Anger never hid in Ryan's expression when he was about to deal, and it had been there. But somehow the circumstance had changed. Drastically. He'd revealed a secret to her. Then told her to walk back. Without seriously hurting her or even drawing blood.

Had Cadence's God done that?

**

Ryan let Annie climb down into the bunker and waited until he saw her step off the stairs before letting Jada fly down behind her. Despite his immortal feelings an hour ago, his body had started to close down. His muscles ached - no, throbbed. He hadn't done a jaunt like that in a long time, and he could almost feel every bruise on his ribs. He started down the stairs and pulled the door closed. Annie stood to the side, stretching over one leg. A putrid odor had spread from his vomit.

"You need to use the washroom before I tie you up?" The sentence sounded cruel.

'Before I tie you up'.

"Why do you have to do that?" She stood and voiced his own question with an incredulous expression. He cracked his neck to each side. *Because Michelle wants to see you suffer. Because she'd kill you if she thought any different. And she asks to see pictures of the scars.*

"Same reason I don't let you two talk when I'm not here. You'd get into trouble. And do I need to remind you that you just tried to run away?" Anger crept across her face again. She sucked in a breath and pressed her lips together. *Good. She was learning not to argue.*

"But you haven't even given us a chance!"

He raised his eyebrows and sighed. "You've got another beating coming your way if you keep up with this. Now do you need the washroom or not?" She let her shoulders slump and scowled up at him. "Hey - you're an athlete, not a drama queen." The insult sunk in and her face hardened.

"I'll use the washroom", she mumbled.

"Okay." He turned to open the door.

"Wait -"

He felt his eyes bulge with the impatience he was trying to hide. "What now?"

"What did you do to my dad?" He rubbed his forehead. Mentioning Simon had been a mistake. There wasn't a quick explanation, not one that wouldn't come with more questions. He ignored her stare.

"We had coffee and talked about how it's hard that you're not at home."

"Oh."

He opened the door and the light shone on Teagan's face. She squinted and looked away. Long brown hair hung around her shoulders. The sprint, chase and capture had helped ease his anger and given him time to think of something painful but not chaotic. He stepped inside and let his shadow fall over her.

"Annie, let's go", he called over his shoulder to where she still stood. "Ten minutes. Get cleaned up, and clean your knees. First Aid stuff is in there."

She sighed and walked past.

"Annie!" Teagan gasped. "You look like... you're okay?"

"Yeah, I'm okay.' She rushed in and knelt beside her. "I'm alright. Are -"

"Washroom or the wall, Annie." He ordered.

"I better go." She stood and bit her lip on her way to the side of the room and shut the door behind her.

Ryan braced against the doorframe and watched Teagan stare at the closed door where her only friend now had gone. After a moment, she turned back to him. He knew as much as any other kid that waiting was often worse than the actual punishment. So, he crossed his arms and waited. And let her tremble.

Only silence sat between them now, and he enjoyed the fact that she was likely terrified that he'd attack her at any moment. She coughed once and tried to cover it, as if the noise had scared her. He finally stepped toward her.

"What you did today put Annie's life in danger", he said, lowering in front of her. She let their eyes meet for a second, but then her expression darted around the room. "You gonna take ownership for that?"

"What are you going to do to me?" She blurted.

"Answer my question."

"I don't know..."

"What do you mean, '*you don't know*'?" He demanded. "What was going through your head?"

She let her eyes flash up at him, but then looked away. "I thought that... I thought she could escape and get help..."

"Listen to me, hey - look at me. Believe it or not, there are people worse than me out there." He noticed that he was wagging his hand at her as he spoke. He stopped and sighed. Look, if either of you leave, you're as good as dead."

"What do you mean?" Her tone was turning rough again already.

"I mean..." He dragged his bag from where it had been laying on the floor. "That this is the safest place for you to be right now." He dug around for a rubber band. The one he'd used this morning to hold the food. He finally found and grabbed his phone too.

"What are you talking about?" Her defiant voice rose, and luckily, he noticed Annie stepping out of the washroom then, or else he might have snapped.

"Against the wall." He ordered, then looked back to Teagan before Annie moved. A way to show he trusted Annie to do what he said. A few seconds later she sat down. "I'll clean the bandages on your arms when I'm finished."

Teagan glanced at her, then continued. "Nobody wants to hurt us except you." He ignored her comment and put the rubber band between his teeth, then pulled her head away from the wall. He started to gather her hair to the top with both hands.

"Don't touch my hair - hey! What are you doing?"

"Teagan, don't argue." Annie's quiet voice. Smart girl. He wrapped Teagan's hair tightly with the rubber band, then grabbed the flashlight to search the floor. He found Jada with the light and she started to wag her tail and trotted up against Ryan.

"There we go." He reached a few feet sideways and picked up his knife. Both girls gasped as the light illuminated it.

"Wait!" Teagan screamed. "What are - Ryan, wait!"

"You're sorry now, huh?" He scoffed. "No. I gave you lots of time to apologize." He started to cut the binds around her feet.

"What? But I'm sorry! Please, I -"

"Let's see: Your first escape attempt, then you broke my nose, and put Annie in danger... sounds like three strikes to me."

They both began to scream. "Ryan, please -"

"I'm sorry!"

"We'll do anything -"

"One more chance -"

"Enough!" He pulled the tape off her jeans. "Get up, Teagan."

"Just me?" Her voice was shaky.

"Yeah, just you."

"Ryan, please..." Annie interjected. She wore her timid look again. Pleading and fearful.

"Stay here." He said to her. "Teagan, let's go." He pulled her up by the arm and pushed her ahead of him, out the door. "Kneel in front of the stairs." He followed her out and closed the door. She continued to stand facing him.

"Ryan..." She'd lost the edge in her voice now. It was barely more than a whisper. "I'm so scared." Her hazel eyes were wet.

"I would be too." He held the knife at his side and turned the handle in his grasp. "But all actions have consequences. You of all people should know that."

"I won't ever fight back again." She whimpered.

"I know." She screwed her face up with emotion as she realized she couldn't get out of this one. He stepped forward and took her arm before she could move. "Down or I'll take you down myself." He saw a hard swallow pass in her throat. Goosebumps formed under his hand. She looked straight ahead for a breath's length, then went down one knee at a time. He let her kneel in silence and wait, while he stood behind her. Eventually she started to cry softly. He took hold of the top of her ponytail, about an inch from the rubber band. "This is for breaking my nose." He ripped the knife through it and she gasped at the sudden release. He straightened and dropped the hair in front of her.

"No... oh my, oh my -" A harsh sob rattled through her body. "You - you -"

"Hey!" He circled to face her. "I could break your bones and believe me, I want to in the worst way, but I'm giving you another chance." He snapped a picture. *Michelle would enjoy this.*

"You - you, monster!" Her pale face had turned red. "You're sick!"

"You think I'm a monster?" He crouched in front of her. "Not yet, princess." He slapped her across the face.

Smack!

She cried out as the motion whipped her head sideways.

"That's for wasting my time. And for being ungrateful." He stood and watched her weep for a few seconds. Then snapped another picture. After he was satisfied, he pulled her up by the arm. "If you ever do something like that again, I'll break your arm."

She refused to look up at him.

No problem.

He pulled her to the door and pushed her back in. Then he grabbed her blanket and threw it out of the room. "So you can think about what you did while you stay awake and shiver until I get back."

"I wish you'd never come back!" He rolled his eyes and taped her mouth shut. He didn't say another word as he cleaned Annie's bandages, but as the silence dragged on, the sound of him hitting Teagan's face began to replay in his memory. Again, and again.

What had he become?

Chapter 12

Throbbing pain ravaged his muscles as Ryan pulled to the curb and shut off the ignition. On the drive home drowsiness had crept in so subtly that his eyes only flashed open when the jeep was inches from the ditch. The morning trip had been a mistake. For so many reasons. He still couldn't believe what he'd done.

'You're a monster!'

Yes. Yes, he was. He rubbed his temples and tried to let go of his thoughts for the time being. Then pushed himself out the door. Jada leapt out the back of his jeep when he lifted the hatch to grab his bag and bike. He rolled his shoulders and heard several bones crack. He needed another hot shower, Gravol, and he desperately needed to get back in bed. He trudged to the front door and stumbled as his vision swam sideways. He caught himself on the railing and took one last deep breath to let go of the morning, before pushing the door open. Jada bounded in ahead of him, but instead of darting around him for attention she ran into the house. Strange. He heard her paws skidding in through the kitchen, then her sounds of affection and excitement. Something more interesting than him was in his house.

He stepped in, closed the door, and braced his bike against the wall. "Jada?"

She tore back across the kitchen and crashed against his legs. She licked at his hands wildly, but then took off again. Ryan narrowed his brows, slid out his knife and hid it behind his leg. Then crept forward to see around the corner.

"Call her off." Wade was sprawled in the love seat with a gun extended.

***

Simon had spent most of the day sorting through memos, labels and various lists on his desk, but somehow hadn't made an iota of progress. His mind had become a hurricane of thoughts, each holding value, and each crashing against the others. Eventually as the afternoon ticked into its later hours, he let his staff know that he needed personal time and left the office.

Now he drove. And considered his recent actions.

The late-night *'hero'* act with Annie's coach. A man whom he had only spoken with on a personal level once before. His confused mind had coerced him into dictating a patient's care without their consent. He should have called an ambulance. Should have taken him to the hospital where a person of the law would surely have questioned him further than he had.

But he had wanted to be useful.

To help someone who meant so much to Annie. It had been too long since he'd taken an interest in the things that were important to her. Her coach was as good a place to start as any. The poor man had been tied up and unconscious. Likely scared out of his mind. But as Simon had lifted him into his truck, Ryan had stirred and began to mumble a string of unconnected phrases:

'Can't stay here... Ann... Teag... no one knows...'

***

"Touch her and I swear I'll rip you apart with my hands." Ryan's words pushed past gritted teeth. Jada, like most huskies, loved all people and wasn't afraid now, but if the scene escalated she'd panic.

"Then call her off." Wade's dark eyes showed that he'd seen death too many times to care about Ryan's threat. Varying colors of bruises covered his face.

"Why didn't you kill me last night? That's what you want."

164

"Kill you?" His face widened in a sarcastic grin, "We've only just started having fun together, baby boy. I couldn't let you get away from me after just one scuffle."

Scuffle, huh? Ryan swallowed. "Jada, let's go." He started down the hall. She glanced his way but continued to hop and sniff. He whistled and motioned for her to follow. She glanced between the men, as if deciding which held more interest. "Jada, come here now!" She whined, but then tore after him toward his bedroom. As soon as she'd followed him in, he slipped out and shut the door. She to bark and scratch the door. Ryan tapped his head against the closed door and tried to think past the pain. He dug his fingers into his palms as his skin burned and he felt another wave of nausea begin... Finally, coming up empty, he pulled out his knife and turned.

The muzzle of Wade's gun pressed into his abs.

"Aw. You seem tense." Wade sneered. He reached behind Ryan's back and found his closed fist. "Hmmm. Let go of it." He held onto Ryan's fingers until the knife released into his hand. "There we go. You okay, pretty boy? Not looking so good." He brought the knife up in front of them to study, and let out a low whistle. "You weren't going to use this on me, were you?

Ryan set his jaw and narrowed his eyes. "I told you: I don't have money."

Wade tilted his head down the hall, then nodded for Ryan to walk ahead of him. "I know what you said, boy. I just had so much fun with you last night, that I thought I'd come by for a visit. I was missing you this morning."

Ryan clenched his teeth together and walked past, as Wade continued.

"You were out cold so fast last night though… I doubt you felt much after that."

Ryan dug his fingernails into his skin.

"Palms open, pretty boy."

Ryan grunted and cast a side glance over his shoulder just in time to see the heel of Wade's boot before it hit him. He hollered as his neck lashed backwards and he crashed to the floor. He turned to attack, but Wade kicked him in the gut. He gasped and landed on his back. With the little strength he had left, he rolled onto his side and pushed away from Wade.

"It felt good, you know. Finally seeing you suffer after all these years." Wade circled and booted him in the chest. Ryan flinched and gasped for air. Wade kicked him in the gut again, and the hit brought another flashback to the shed - to James and the rope. Ryan's vision turned black, then light, and then black again. The room grew hot. Blurry splotches faded in and out around him. "Let's have some more fun." Wade dropped to his knees and grabbed Ryan's t-shirt.

"Get away from me!" Ryan thrashed his arms as Wade pulled his t-shirt off. "What the hell are -" Wade punched him hard in the gut. Twice. Ryan flinched and groaned, and the t-shirt went over his head. "Hey!" Wade twisted the material around his wrists, so his arms hung above him. Ryan fought to free himself, but Wade hit him again, then straddled him "You can't run anymore, boy!" He grabbed Ryan's head and bashed it against the wooden floor.

Black. White. Black.

"James told me about your little art collection." Wade whispered hoarsely and flicked the knife in front of Ryan's eyes.

"Get out of my house!" Ryan jabbed his wrists backward and managed to hit Wade's chin.

"No can do, baby! I'm going to leave my mark!" He dug the knife into Ryan's biceps and dragged it down his skin.

"Stop!" He screeched. *No, no, no!* "AHHH!" His voice cracked. He squeezed his eyes shut and tried to take it.

Black. White. Hot. He faded out, then back, and felt like he'd been slapped with a raging wall of heat.

"You like that, pretty boy?" Wade snarled. He pulled the knife out and started a new cut. "You'll never forget your past now, will you?"

Ryan swore and choked. He tried to reach up to grab Wade's face. "Get off - No, stop!" Wade pulled the knife down his arm again. Ryan tried to scream as another burst of heat came from behind his forehead, then the room turned black. His body seemed to be falling.

***

Alec cracked his neck and threw back the glass of rye. He wiped his freshly shaven face. "How's our boy, Ryan?"

"He's gutless, as I expected he might be."

He grunted and drank again. "You're prepared to take care of them if he doesn't?"

"Of course."

"And no one has caught onto your involvement?"

"Don't be ridiculous. I haven't done a thing except pass on your requests."

"And Simon?"

"Oh, don't worry about him. We'll take everything and leave him to die alone. Just like he did to you." Michelle lit a cigarette and rubbed the back of her neck. Alec poured himself another glass.

"I've waited too long for this."

"We both have."

***

'Get your act together! Clean out the shed! You think those weights will make you a better person? You're nothing! Come here, and I'll show you what a strong man looks like!'

Ryan shot up, soaked in sweat. His bare chest shivered. The house was silent. He searched the floor with his palms. Was he alone?

168

He tried to look in all directions at once. Then pain roared from his arm. His blood-soaked t-shirt was wrapped around the wounds. He gaped at the amount of blood. And fainted.

A few minutes later he shot up again. This time he staggered to his feet and spun to determine if he was alone. He'd been left alive again. Even bandaged so he wouldn't bleed out.

Wade didn't want him to die.

The bloodied knife lay on the floor. He snatched it up and continued to turn. His balance slipped and he half-landed on the arm of his sofa. He righted himself and lumbered through his home looking for Wade. Loud barking came from his bedroom. Jada was alive too. He started for his room, but a burst of heat beneath his skin made him decide to help himself first. He slogged to the kitchen sink and ducked his head under the faucet. The cold liquid soaked his head and ran down his neck, refreshing his skin. He turned and sucked the water like an animal, then choked and sputtered. He braced himself on the counter and took heavy breaths. Jada's barking continued. He splashed his face once more, then moved the short distance to his room and opened the door. Jada barrelled into him, pushing her nose against his legs frantically. She jumped and leaned her paws against him to look at his face.

"It's okay, girl." He painfully made his way down to the floor and massaged her ears. He tried to look brave. She tore away and ran through the house barking, looking for Wade. Then came back a moment later to look him over before taking off again. Finally, she pushed up against him and he held her for what seemed an eternity.

Finally, Ryan stood and moved into his kitchen for more water. He leaned on the counter and chugged a glass in seconds, refilled it and did it again. Only days ago, a promising future had been within his reach. But now his own home had become dangerous and life was pushing his hand to play a turn he didn't want to make. Having Wade thrown in prison would come at the cost of his own freedom, and with his luck he'd probably end up as his cellmate.

Or he could kill again.

No!

That or jail.

See? You can't escape your past!

Events he'd set in motion so long ago still followed him. No escape. He dropped his chin to his chest. A big sigh left his lips and he rubbed his temples.

Those events don't define you.

Where had that thought come from? It was as if a voice from outside of him. And it was right. He'd changed. And now devoted his life to helping others change for the better.

Maybe the cops should hear his side of the story first.

He winced at the itching and shooting pain from within the gashes, and imagined several muscles had been cut. He'd never do something like this to another human. Though now thinking back, he wasn't sure whether this was worse than the scars he'd carved into his parents and Wade's brother. The scars were shallow at first, but once his father gained consciousness and began to berate him, Ryan had cut to draw blood. He'd only wanted to overpower them, escape, then turn them in. But as he'd mulled over his options he watched infection and blood loss kill them slowly. And after they'd passed there was no way back.

He swallowed and shook his head to clear the images. He drank another full glass of water. He was a new person now. The past was the past.

"Why are Annie and Teagan victims of your past?"

Hey -!

He glanced over his shoulder, then around the kitchen. Where was this voice coming from? Never had his inner thoughts seemed so loud and clear. He swallowed again.

'Victims of his past.' No, they weren't. They were part of an elaborate scenario. And he was the one to remove them from the danger. He was protecting them.

"You know you're dangerous!"

He set the glass down.

I could be a lot worse though. Like Alec.

He turned on the faucet, hoping the running water would wash the images away. But they came anyway. Annie's tears. Teagan throwing up from pain. Annie's screams when he slashed her un-medicated arm. Slapping Teagan. Locking them in the dark. In the cold. His crooked past had crossed into these two unsuspecting, young lives

171

and he'd punished them both for trying to escape. He pressed the bottom of his palms against his eyes. He wasn't a hero. His domineering nature had basically turned him into a sadist.

He looked at the bloodied material wrapped around his arm and choked on rising tears. Panic began to build in his mind, the same way it had thirteen years ago. More images of the girls seared his memory: their scared eyes, whimpers, pleas for warmth... He started to shake. He noticed the heat in his face first; burning his cheeks, then spreading down into his chest. Shame. Remorse. His vision blurred with tears.

He had thought he could still be a leader to them. That one day they'd respect him and be grateful that he saved them from Michelle's plans and Simon's potential future plans. But who was the worse evil in this situation? Him or Simon? Or Michelle?

He was. And Teagan and Annie were paying for his secrets.

He slid down the wall and began to weep. Any remaining hope for redemption left him. He choked on jagged breaths and cried into his hands. Jada pushed against him and licked at the tears. He wrapped his good arm around her and shook with sobs.

J. M. Bergman

Chapter 13

About twenty minutes later, Ryan accepted that he needed medical attention. He wrapped real bandaging over the bloody t-shirt, pulled on a tank top and rode his bike to an emergency clinic. A motherly African-American nurse, named Patti, took care of him. She gave him medication and cream for the swelling on his face and bruises on the rest of his body. X-rays showed that his ribs hadn't been broken in either fight. Badly bruised, yes. He called the incident gang violence. Patti saw through the lie, but she couldn't pry answers from him. He'd been a lock without a key for decades.

A cop dropped in to take a statement and Ryan made something up to the effect of it being a 'random attack' on the street. That he'd been knocked out cold almost instantly and couldn't remember what happened. A blow to his pride for sure, but it was the easiest way out.

After the stitches to his arm, and to the dismay of the doctor and nurses, he insisted on going home. Patti slipped him her home phone number, saying that her husband, Morgan, could take care of whoever was causing him trouble. She called a cab for him and his bike, and asked again if she could call the police to watch his house.

"I'll do it when I get home." He winked. "Promise." She'd crossed her arms and shook her head with a look that said she didn't believe him, but stopped fussing. As he rode home in silence, his medicated body became drowsy. There was no way he'd make it back to the bunker tonight. He wouldn't be able to face the girls anyway. Once home, he managed to amble up the stairs to his door, fall onto the couch and speed-dial Michelle. "Hey. Just back from the hospital. Can you come over and make sure I'm still alive in an hour?"

"Ryan? What -"

"Please."

She hesitated. "Of course. Get some rest, I'll be there soon." He tossed his phone to the floor where Jada sat watching him, then stretched out on the couch and his dreams took him.

***

A gust of wind blew leaves across Simon's windshield. The windshield wipers took them away and cleared the raindrops from a light drizzle which had started. He was still thinking about Ryan. Something about that young man's eyes had made him uneasy. His injuries were more than a random act of violence. And why would he mention his daughter unless the two incidents were connected? If this

175

were true, it would be crucial for him to go to the police with the information. But Ryan held that he didn't remember enough to say anything of value.

His phone suddenly vibrated, breaking his thoughts. *Lydia.* "Hi, Lydia."

"Are you coming home for dinner tonight?"

He glanced at the time - it was well after 6:00 PM. He sighed and absently rubbed his hand over his forehead. He'd been driving for hours. "No, I don't think so. I just need to - drive. And think." Silence came through the line.

"That's something we can do together, isn't it?" A sharp comment. That was deserved, he supposed. They hadn't spent time together in days and he'd purposefully been staying away until the wee hours of the morning, trying to make sense of recent events.

"I need to be alone. And I need you to understand that." He snapped with an edge of his own, which had unfortunately become a more common occurrence. He regretted it immediately. "Is there something I can get you while I'm out?"

"How long will you be?" Avoiding his offer.

"I don't know. I'll try and be home by nine, okay?" A moment of hesitation passed by. He hadn't told her about hosting a patient in their home. Or about how he now drove the streets looking for people to help. She wouldn't understand and would probably tell him to focus his grief in more hours at the hospital. Or maybe not. "I'm thinking of dropping by to see Annie's coach." He blurted.

"You're doing what?" *Not an understanding voice.*

"Why is that such a bad idea?"

"You don't know the man, Simon...what are you expecting? A personal training session in therapy?"

"No, of course not -"

"He's not even a friend of the family! He's young. You can't expect him to know how to talk with a grieving father."

Simon's temperature rose. "I'm not grieving yet, Lydia. Annie's coming home."

"That's not what I meant." They both became silent for a moment. "You can talk to me for support, Simon."

"We can talk if you're awake when I get home."

"Fine. I'll leave your supper in the fridge."

"Thanks, Lydia." Click. Well, that took care of one idea. He'd spend the evening alone, thinking. He sighed and put his vehicle back in gear.

***

"I love it." Michelle beamed and glanced up from the latest photo on his phone of Teagan's tear-streaked face and short hair. *Joy at Teagan's suffering.* Inhuman. How had he missed that? Teagan served as a third party to all this and Michelle had no personal reason to hate her, but she did. He'd tried to decide if this were true between fits of sleep since he'd gotten home. And now that he realized how awful Michelle was, he began to plan his future without her. Starting tomorrow. After he became rich.

"The ransom is set to be dropped off in the morning. You're ready, right babe?"

"Yeah." Ryan stirred beef stew on the stove and sipped from a mug in his other hand. "I still don't think I should have to be there. I've already done my part." *I became a criminal for you.* He set the spoon on the stove and leaned against the counter in his black track pants and a thin gray sweater. He took another sip of tea. "My face won't be completely healed by tomorrow either, so there's no way I can blend in at the train station."

"Babe", Michelle rose from the wooden dinner table. "You look great." She walked her fingers walked up his chest as she spoke. "I wouldn't trust this to any other person."

He looked down into her alluring turquoise eyes and sipped from his mug again. "Then I want more than half." She stepped back fast, as he expected she might. Her expression looked ready to kill him and he wondered if it was safe to continue. But it was now or never. "I've done unforgivable things for you and Alec."

"Excuse me? Simon is the unforgivable one!"

"I know. But I'm doing some unforgivable things too." He crossed his arms. "I hit Teagan today...right before I took that picture." He dropped his gaze to the floor and stared at his bare feet. "I've become something terrible."

"Well she wouldn't be alive to mess with your conscience if you'd just listened to us and followed the plan to begin with!" Ryan snapped his gaze back up and saw only a merciless expression in Michelle's eyes. Two innocent teenagers could die because of her connections to them and she probably wouldn't even shed a tear. He cracked his neck to distract himself from asking her how she could sleep at night. "Simon is a killer! Do you not understand what I've been telling you? A life for a life!"

"What about Teagan's life? She has nothing to do with this!"

"You know we needed to take her so the connection to Simon isn't obvious." Michelle retorted, then raked her hand through her wavy hair.

"So, let's give her back after the money comes in tomorrow. Simon would still be without his daughter."

"And let her talk? Sometimes I question your intelligence!"

He clenched his teeth together and let out a long breath. Irritation was building inside him. "Teagan had nothing to do with the death of Alec's wife. She's innocent."

"Innocent?" Michelle spat. "Look me in the eye and tell me you haven't considered killing her." He narrowed his eyes at her. "Thought so. We'll be doing her parents a favor."

He scratched the back of his neck. "Look: Simon's wife is dead and now you took his daughter. Tomorrow you'll have his money too. He'll have nothing left, which means you're square. Killing Teagan is just as bad as what he did."

179

She slapped him, hard. "Take that back, you bastard!"

He stood, shocked, and clenched his fists at his side. Who did this woman think she was? Because she sure wasn't invincible. He could take her down. Right here. He was a criminal after all. He refused to look at her until the stinging had passed; then he cleared his throat and stepped forward, pressing against her.

"Hold on, babe..." She pushed back, the same way Annie had tried to stop him right before he hurt her. He grabbed Michelle's wrists and backed her into the wall. "Ryan, stop! I was thinking about the baby!" She gasped and ducked in case he swung at her.

Right. The baby. The reason for this whole twisted game. He glared upward and clenched his teeth.

"Babe, we're in this together, right? All or nothing?" She stared up at him, and he dropped her hands without looking at her and went back to the stove.

'All or nothing'? He'd erase this entire relationship if he could. Then he'd have nothing to do with this maniacal woman and her brother. But then Teagan and Annie would be dead already. He stirred the stew, then took a sip from the spoon.

More salt.

He'd known sleeping with another man's wife could have consequences. But Michelle's interest in him had made him feel new masculinity and value. The way she'd chosen *him* out of all the men at her fingertips.

They'd spent sporadic nights together and somehow, she'd unlocked his long-kept secrets. He pushed her away at first, but she seduced him into sharing - said it only seemed fair. Their relationship was a secret from her husband, after all, so she deserved to know his dark secret too. He started small and hadn't intended to tell her everything. But there was freedom in releasing his secret, and she was a good listener.

But sharing came with huge consequences. And it made sense why she'd chosen him.

Her intentions became clear a few days later when she laid out the murder-ransom scheme. At first, he laughed at her. 'Normal' people don't come up with plans like that. But then she demanded his involvement in exchange for not revealing his past to the police. He'd never felt so betrayed and nearly sent his fist through the bedroom wall.

They'd argued on and off for days. Finally, he persuaded her that he'd abduct the girls and make them disappear. Forever. To Simon, it would be the same as if Annie were dead. Eventually, Michelle had agreed and this unending nightmare had begun.

He shook salt and pepper into the boiling pot.

But simply kidnapping and hiding them was much different than what had happened so far. As soon as the money came in tomorrow he'd tell them everything and hope they could somehow forgive him. Apologizing wouldn't cover what he'd done to them. He knew that. But in this moment, he decided that he'd spend the rest of his life making up for his mistakes if he had to, and with his half of the ransom he'd make life comfortable for the three of them. If the girls wanted, they could leave the city. Maybe even the country. Start over with new identities. Somewhere above ground.

Or you could tell the police what happened to you as a child and what you did to escape. And then turn in Alec and Michelle.

The clear voice from before. He closed his eyes and considered it. Alec and Michelle would go to prison and Annie and Teagan could go home. But he would rot in jail. He rubbed the back of his neck. No, not an option. He'd worked too hard to get to where he was in life now. He glanced over his shoulder. Michelle was staring at him.

"Yeah, all or nothing." He pressed his lips against her forehead.

***

Saturday

4:45 AM

Ryan lay beneath his thin blanket, twisting violently in his sleep. The way he did every night when the nightmares came.

Shadows sprawled long over the yard. The sun dipped below the horizon. His parents were dragging two kicking bodies across the yard to the trees where the dead were buried. But these weren't little boys.

Annie and Teagan!

He lurched forward to free them - but the ropes held him to a tree. The same tree they tied him to every time he tried to make a rescue attempt. "Teagan! Annie! NO!"

He bolted upright, soaked in sweat, and gasped for air. He closed his eyes and focused on breathing through the next few moments. It had been a dream. A dream. The digital clock read 4:47 AM. Four hours until his first client at the gym. Then the big finale of picking up the ransom. The end was in sight. And if he left now he'd have enough time to make it out to the bunker and perhaps he could start to make peace with the girls.

He took one last intentional breath and kicked his legs off the bed. The cool floor sent a shiver up his spine. He slapped his face to get fully awake, then stood. He felt much better than last night. He cracked his neck and fingers. Then walked past a window to the dresser. He jerked back for a double-take.

Frost.

"Damn." He bolted to his closet, dressed and grabbed a couple extra sweaters and socks. As he ran to the kitchen he snagged his backpack off the bathroom floor
and stuffed the clothes inside. Then stuck leftover stew from the fridge into the microwave. He swept his hands through his hair, turned and almost tripped over Jada, then turned his kettle on and grabbed for thermoses.

What time had the ground frozen? It would take forty-five minutes to reach the woods and another half hour to run or bike to the bunker.

They might already be dead.

He set the thermoses on the table and rushed back down the hallway. One thermos crashed to the floor behind him and he jumped, still skittish from his nightmare. He threw open the closet door and scanned everything he could take in. He grabbed bottles of cold medicine and a sleeping bag.

***

After speeding, because it was necessary, he and Jada arrived at the bunker with his bike and backpack of supplies just over an hour later. The trees glistened beneath hoarfrost and his cheeks were numb from sweat and the cool air. He pulled the hatch open and his fingers burned from the touch of the ice-cold metal. He hurried down after Jada and flipped on the overhead lights. He breathed a fog of condensation into his hands. "Stay." He pointed to the place she always lay to wait for him. He inserted his key into the lock on their door.

Light shone to the back wall, where they both appeared to be sleeping. Neither one moved to acknowledge his presence. A dim light which he'd never used before hung from the ceiling and he turned it on, wondering what he'd been thinking this whole time by not using it.

Dark deeds were better done in darkness.

He realized now how twisted his mind had become. He hurried forward to kneel in front of them. Teagan's bare arms were pale. He refused to look for a pulse. He unzipped his backpack, pulled out the sleeping bag and wrapped it around both girls.

"Hey -" He rubbed Teagan's arms. Her skin was very cold. He carefully pulled the duct tape off her face but she didn't flinch. *Wake up!* He still couldn't tell if she was breathing. He did the same thing to Annie's face. Then held her head with one hand and shook her shoulder with the other. Her head dropped back to her chest.

Color drained out of his face. *No, no, no….*

"Come on..." He pulled Annie away from the wall and rubbed her sides vigorously. "Annie!" He shouted. Her head hung and wobbled with the movement. He rubbed harder, faster. "Jeffreys, wake up!" A small noise escaped and he grabbed her face and looked for a sign of life. He pried one eye open to check her pupil. Another tiny sound of protest and this time he knew it came from her lips. "Annie? Kid, can you hear me?" He kept rubbing her sides. Her eyes fluttered open. "Hey, say something. Can you hear me?" But she moaned and closed her eyes again. "Hey! Stay with me." He took hold of her face and tried speaking to her again. He grabbed his knife and cut her hands free. "Annie, come on, say something!" He continued to move. Finally, he noticed her move a little beneath the sleeping bag. He stopped and lifted her head again. Her eyes were partially open with a blank expression. "Annie, what's my name?"

She blinked. Her pupils locked on him then, noticing him. She stared absently. Different expressions crossed her eyes.

Recognition. Confusion. Then sadness.

"What's my name, Annie?" He repeated.

She frowned. "I remember, Ryan." Defeat and betrayal again. She closed her hands around the edge of the sleeping bag and tugged it closer.

"I need you to rub your sides to stay warm, okay? I have some warm food to give you in a minute." He cut her feet loose too, and helped her fold her legs up against her. "Try and keep your legs moving, okay?" She'd be alright. He focused back on Teagan. He ripped off his windbreaker, then yanked off his blue hooded sweater and pulled it down over her head. Then turned her away from him, pulled her up onto his knees, hugged her from behind, and vigorously rubbed her sides.

"Ryan?" It was Annie's soft voice. "Your arms…"

He closed his eyes. The new scars and stitches. Not something he felt like explaining right now. "Don't worry about it, kid. What you do to people, comes right back at you, I guess. You remember me talking about that on the field?" He offered a sheepish grin. She either ignored his statement or didn't understand what he'd said, because she continued to stare blankly. "Keep your arms and legs moving, alright?"

He kept warming Teagan's core and tried to keep an eye on Annie at the same time. What seemed like an eternity passed, and there was still no response. *No…* He shut his eyes.

186

"What is it?" Annie's weak, scared voice. "She's okay, right?"

He couldn't look at her. Not when this was his fault. All his fault.

"Ryan!"

"I don't know!" He snapped back, and caught himself, before looking away and sighing. "I don't know." He turned Teagan around and searched for a pulse. Nothing. He used two fingers and tried another spot on her neck. Still nothing. He heard Annie gasp and start to make the sounds he knew too well.

The disbelief that someone close to you had died.

No! They were both supposed to be safe here! This should have been a place of refuge! He moved his fingers again, then hesitated...

Yes! A faint pulse. He freed her arms and laid her on the ground. He began fast chest compressions, tilted her head, and watched for movement. Then he opened her mouth and gave two breaths. Still nothing. He began the chest compressions again. Annie was kneeling beside them now.

"Teagan, wake up!" Her voice cracked. "Teagan! Teagan!"

Ryan pumped Teagan's chest and knew it wouldn't be much longer before he broke something. But there was nothing else he could do. Annie was crying, still pleading at Teagan's body. He stopped and gave two more breaths, then back to compressions. Tears began to blur his vision.

Please... please... God, don't let her die...

Teagan coughed and tried to lift her head.

"Teagan? Can you hear me?" He studied her tilted face. She wasn't responding and her torso started to tip forward. He caught her with his other hand. "Teagan, listen to me." Her head dropped. "Teagan!" He started earnestly rubbing her torso again. "Annie! I need one of the thermoses from my bag. Do you think you can grab one and bring it to me?"

She followed his gaze. "Okay", she whispered. She crawled forward, the blanket slipping off her body as she did, and reached into the bag. The thermoses were both heavy and she needed both arms to retrieve one. But she did it.

"Thanks." He leaned forward and closing the distance between them, and took the thermos from her hands. Her face was streaked with tears. "Do you think you can drink from the other thermos? It'll warm you up." He watched her consider it. "There are big socks in there too. Put them on." He knelt back in front of Teagan and opened the thermos. It was the tea he had made. Using the cup, that acted as a second lid, he poured out a small amount, and held Teagan's head with his other hand. He held the cup at her mouth for several seconds to allow the steam to touch her lips first. Finally, she made a small noise and he noticed her eyes crack open slightly. He pressed the cup gently against her lips until she accepted a small amount. He waited until she swallowed, then offered it to her again. She'd recover, but she needed lots of attention. They both did. He noticed then that Annie was still sitting beside his backpack; she had found socks, and it looked like she was trying to take off a shoe. Okay, he'd have to take care of her first so she could help

188

him with Teagan. He also needed to call work and to do that he'd need to get outside and find a signal.

"Annie, come here." She glanced up at him. "I want you back here in the blanket beside Teagan." He motioned with the cup in his hand. "I'll help you with those socks."

"Okay." She crawled forward with the socks dragging from one hand.

"Give me your hand." He set down the cup and they reached for each other at the same time, and he pulled her forward. "Okay, sit up tall. Good. I'm going to lean Teagan on your shoulder, okay? You'll both be warmer that way." Annie put her arm around Teagan and looked at him again. "Good, good." Ryan grabbed the sleeping bag and wrapped it around both girls, then quickly went to untying her shoes. "I don't know why you ladies wear trendy stuff like this", he muttered, sliding one of her feet out and pulling a thick, grey sock over it and up her shins. "They have no support." He pulled her other foot out and did the same with the other sock. These were the socks he used for running on extremely cold days and he knew they would help. "How's that?" He asked, as he helped slide her feet back into the shoes. He grabbed another sweater from his bag and pulled it over her body before she could respond.

"Thank you." She closed her eyes.

"Yeah. Annie, you need to stay awake for now, okay?" He reached for his thermos again and poured the steaming liquid into the cup. She was reaching forward to take it. "No, no, you hold onto

Teagan, I'll help you drink this. Small sips, it's hot." He moved closer and introduced the hot liquid in the same way he had with Teagan. Her eyes grew as the steam touched her skin. She put her mouth around the cup's brim eagerly, but he didn't tip the liquid for her yet. "Not too fast, it's hot." Then let her drink. She swallowed and immediately parted her lips again, this time not pulling back until he gave her a more than last time. "There you go, good." He continued this for a couple minutes.

Finally, she pulled back and dabbed her mouth with the sleeve of his sweater that she now wore. "Thanks."

"You're welcome." He grabbed the second thermos, along with a pair of socks for Teagan. He started to cut the tape around Teagan's ankles so he could get her into big socks. "Annie, listen to me: I never meant for you ladies to get hurt like this." He couldn't bring himself to look at her. She didn't say anything. "I -" He started, paused, then tried again. "Taking you was a difficult decision. One I would have never made under different circumstances." He slid Teagan's foot out of her shoe and slid on a sock.

"Can we go home now?" Her voice was so soft he almost missed it.

He stopped moving for a moment. "No, Annie, you can't." He said in a tone which meant there would be no further discussing. "There are things you don't understand. I'll explain soon, I promise." He pulled the second sock up, slipped Teagan's shoes back on and rewrapped her legs in the blanket. "Okay, I have to go outside and make arrangements for work today. I'm going to leave you two just like this so you can keep each other warm. And -" He put his fingers to his mouth and whistled. Jada bolted into the room and jumped on all three of them in turn. "Good girl." He rustled her ears with both his hands, then pointed to the girls with his finger and chin. She leapt into their laps and began moving to find a comfortable position. "She'll keep you warm. Please stay here, drink as much of the tea as you want. I'll be right back. Got it?"

Annie stared back at him blankly. Teagan had closed her eyes again.

"Teagan!" She partially opened her eyes. "Annie, keep her awake, okay? I won't be long." Annie nodded. "Okay." He rubbed Jada's ears, took one more look at the girls and headed back out.

Chapter 14

What is going on with Ryan? Annie thought to herself.

Yesterday he probably would have thrown them both in a river if he could. But now he seemed to care about their well-being. Which was weird. In real life, as he would say, people generally don't cut, beat up or starve the ones they care about. Or show that level of kindness to prisoners. The Ryan Grey she saw in the forest yesterday was very different than the man who had coached her in soccer. And different from who he seemed to be a few days ago. He had hit her. Hurt her. And somehow broke her heart again even though she didn't have much of it left. It still hurt.

What kind of 'circumstances' was he talking about? And why wouldn't he explain his role as the 'good guy'? It's not like she could get away and tell anyone else. He'd made that completely clear. Her escape aside, why on earth had he been in her home? With her father.

And using her mom's favorite mug. There just seemed to be too many misshapen pieces to this puzzle. And why did he care if Teagan lived or died? She'd honestly thought he would kill her yesterday, and he'd almost made her freeze to death by taking her blanket last night. They both could have died down here.

She sucked in a broken breath and pressed her head against Teagan's shoulder.

Jada shifted on their laps and settled back with her head down. Annie remembered the scars on Ryan's arm then. Fresh with stitches. Something dark was haunting him. For months, she'd known that he carried a heavy secret. Occasionally a dark presence would flash across his eyes on the field and he'd seemed to drift away for a slight moment. She'd brought it up once and he snapped something to the effect of, *'We're not here to talk about feelings!'*

She'd never mentioned it again.

But Cadence did.

Cadence. The girl who believed in miracles. And believed in a God who cared about her small life. And every other life, in fact. That's what she had said once. It had been after practise one day when Annie mentioned missing her mom. Cadence had asked if her mom believed in God. Yes, she had believed. She even read Annie stories from the same kind of Bible that Cadence read. Cadence had told her then that her mom was in a heavenly home now. With God. And that Annie would see her again one day if she believed that Jesus forgave her sins. At that time Annie wanted nothing else but to be in that place with her

193

mom. But then the questions about why God would allow her mom to die came. And that had been the end of her thoughts about any kind of faith.

But Cadence never gave up. *'God can help you heal.'* That's what she had said. *'He cares about you. You're not alone. You'll never be alone.'*

But what about now? Where is He, Cadence?

"I'm right here."

Her head spun. The doorway was open, but the room beyond was still empty. Where had the voice come from? Not Teagan. She looked at the doorway again but somehow knew nothing would be there. She felt a strange, warm tingling in her chest,

"I'm right here."

Could it be? Cadence's God?

"I'm your God too."

She choked down a sob. He was talking to her... He could hear her thoughts! A peace, like another blanket, draped over her with that realization. Her mom had died, but she'd died believing God loved her. Annie pondered and swallowed again. She rubbed Teagan's back absently.

"Hey, are you awake?" She spoke softly and Teagan groaned. "Are you warm? I can try and get some of that tea for you."

Teagan shook her head against Annie's shoulder. "He seemed different." Her thin voice held an inkling of hope. Annie reached for her hand and squeezed it.

"I think so too. I just don't understand why."

Teagan squeezed back. They were silent for a moment. Then Teagan spoke again. "How are you, Jada?" She stroked the beautiful dog's white and gray fur and received licks of approval on her arm. "You'll take care of us, right?"

***

"Jake? Hey, I need a last-minute favor." Ryan had walked about fifty feet into the morning darkness outside before he found a signal. Frost glittered from overhanging branches and crisp grass crunched beneath his feet. He rubbed his reddening arms and reprimanded himself for not grabbing a sweater. His white tank-top at least covered his core.

"Hey, man. Whad-d-ya need?" Jake yawned through the receiver. They had met at the gym years back. Most clients requested him or Jake for their personal trainer and the two had become friends through working the same hours so often.

"I'm in a jam for time this morning. Could you take my 9:00 and 9:45 at the gym? Basic core strengthening."

"Yeah, man, for sure. I'm going in early for conditioning anyway. Which clients?"

"Two young guys: Kyle and Jerrid."

"You got it, man."

"Thanks, I owe you." He hung up and scrolled through his contacts for another name. A sharp breeze shot over his arms. He shivered and caught the smell of pine needles. The line picked up after five rings. A long hesitation followed. Ryan searched the ground and pressed his ear against his phone. "Hello?" He tried, when still nothing came through. Finally, a groggy voice spoke.

"Hello?" Hazy and confused.

"Come on, Jeff, it's already 6:30." *How could people still be asleep at this time?*

"Well -" He yawned. "Good morning to you, too."

Ryan rubbed his forehead and shut his eyes. "Jeff, you remember what's happening today, right?"

"Of course…" He drawled. "The briefcase. At ten o'clock -"

"Eleven o'clock!"

"Right. Eleven. Hours from now, though. You thought I forgot, or what?"

Ryan sighed. He took a breath before continuing. "No - I need you to listen closely, okay?"

"Go ahead, I'm listening." He yawned into the receiver again.

Ryan swallowed and debated asking Jeff to repeat what he'd just said, but decided to keep going. "Look, something big has come up. I can't be there -"

"What?" Jeff's voice rose. "You've drilled me for weeks to keep this commitment, and now you're backing out?"

Perhaps he should have led with that statement. At least he knew Jeff understood him. "It's a medical emergency. I don't have time to explain." Another chilled gust whipped around him. "Look, you and Sam are solid. You guys do your thing like we planned, alright?"

"Okay…" Jeff waited for him to continue.

"Is your cousin free this morning?" Ryan held his breath. They needed the third person. To break up the connections and make sure no one traced the money to his house.

"Freddie?" He heard Jeff chuckle. "Oh yeah, I'm sure he's around. You're okay with him handling that last step?"

"You three are the only ones I trust. I'd ask you to do it, but I need you to be the first contact."

Jeff mused. "Well, I'm sure it'll work out. Freddie likes to feel productive."

Ryan pinched the bridge of his nose, then rubbed his neck, trying to keep his voice calm. "Jeff, this is serious, I need -"

"Don't worry about it. I'll promise him lunch and he'll be there." He paused. "You owe me big though, man. Waking me up at this unearthly hour to say you can't make it to your own gig."

"Okay. Thanks. You remember where I hid the key to my front door?"

"I got this, I'll let Fred know. Don't worry, alright?"

Ryan finished the call and hung up. He jogged back towards the bunker.

***

Alec meticulously loaded a bullet into each chamber of his revolver and flicked it shut. All the years of planning leading up to this would finally pay off. Simon's daughter would die today. And vengeance would be sweet. He'd make sure she died slowly. He might kill the doctor too, but that would be decided after forcing him to look at pictures of her dead body. Or perhaps a video would do the job better. If Simon fell apart, he could live. Stay alive with the images haunting the rest of his waking moments. His life would spiral down into depression and self-loathing, and no one would ask questions when his marriage fell apart shortly after. But if he closed down and shut out his emotions, then Alec would kill him too. And enjoy every second of watching him die.

Just like when he'd killed Simon's wife, Maria, almost a decade ago.

Sure, the 'accident' involved vehicles. A hit and run, by yours truly. He'd smashed into the passenger side of the taxi she was in and left her to die. The news stated later that she'd passed away in the hospital that night. The same hospital where his own pregnant wife had died only a week before.

It was the fair thing to do.

Alec's beautiful wife, Beverly, had been in and out of the hospital for weeks, due to a rare condition during her pregnancy. One with no known cures. Their unborn son was going to die in her womb.

198

But they got the good news that an up and coming doctor was developing what experts believed could be a breakthrough medication. This man met with them and had the audacity to assure them that his work could save their son.

Bev would be the first of many to receive the treatment and students would be documenting the process. They were asked to sign waivers if they agreed. Alec had hesitated, but the young doctor had gotten inside Bev's mind and she insisted they go through with it. The treatment kept her hospitalized and between work and visiting hours Alec didn't see much of the doctor again. It was a short trial. The drug destroyed her body in three weeks. She'd passed away with her dying hand in his. Of course, the medical staff were sorry. And the students were sympathetic. But the doctor disappeared into more research. That's what the nurses and the support staff said.

So, Alec mourned the loss alone. And began plotting his revenge.

He'd planned to killed Simon's daughter that day too, but at the last minute, decided to wait. Wait to see if Dr. Jeffreys made his riches in the medical field, and then find a way to take tangible payment for what he had done to him. And now, here they were. It had taken years of watching Simon from a distance, and then getting closer to learn more about him and what he valued. The two men had even spoken face to face in recent years.

But Simon had forgotten him. Forgotten Beverly. Forgotten their son.

199

And now life as Simon knew it would end.

***

Teagan heard Ryan coming down the stairs.

Thump, thump, thump.

Jada leapt off her lap and dashed through the door to meet him, as if he were some celebrity. Yesterday he'd hit her. Hard. And taken one of the few things she valued about her appearance. As a child, when she felt broken inside, her mom would tell her that the world around them was still beautiful. And that she was beautiful too. That the two of them had been gifted with the beauty of long, lush hair. And that if she took care of her outer beauty, she'd eventually feel better inside too.

Down here in this cold dungeon, her hair had curled around her arms and shoulders, the same way her mom used to hold her as a child. It had been the only physical connection to home that she had left. And then he took it from her.

After Annie's escape attempt, she knew the truth: They would never get away from him. And now she wished she could be dead so she could escape from him, and that he had let her die today instead of reviving her. But for whatever twisted reason, he wanted her alive. Probably to prove that he was capable of breaking her and bringing her back at will. That he could force her to obey his authority, and that she could only get away by dying if he allowed it.

She snarled as he approached. If she could move, she'd be waiting around the corner to attack him. To kick him in the groin. Of course, he'd eventually overpower her, and whatever he did to her afterwards would hurt - but why not? He'd keep cutting her regardless of what she did. So, he deserved to feel pain too.

He walked into their cell, and she glared up at him, waiting for some sort of reproach or taunt. Maybe now that she was awake he'd cut her up some more with his knife. Or shave her head. But he didn't come to where she and Annie sat. Instead he went into the washroom. She heard him flick the light switch on, then running water. Every sound seemed magnified. She closed her eyes and tried to drown out the noise. Her chilled body ached. The footsteps drew close now.

"Hey, how are you two holding up?" She heard his voice as if her head were underwater. A wave of hot and cold swept over her and she groaned. For an instant, it felt as though her body was falling forward through the floor. She groaned again and tried to grasp at something solid. Annie must have grabbed her hand, because coolness spread through her arm and she felt herself coming back to the room. After a moment, she allowed her eyelids to flutter open. Annie was holding her hand, but beyond that all she saw was shadowy shapes. His silhouette moved nearby. Liquid gushed from somewhere. He spoke again. "Annie, I have food for you. It's warm and it'll build your strength back up. Then I have some medicine for you to take, okay?"

Annie adjusted her body against her side, then settled again. Smells of beef, vegetables, and barley wafted near her face. Suddenly the gushing sound again, as if a wall of water was crashing toward -

"- gan. Teagan!"

She gasped as light crashed against with a wave of heat inside her body, and she heard his heavy voice. Warmth spread from her knee. She looked down. Ryan's hand shook her knee. His face came into her view. He looked concerned. Not angry. Not upset.

"I'm - I'm awake." She managed, blinking several times.

"Jada." She heard him say as the light faded back to dark shapes and colors. Suddenly Jada's warm tongue licked her face. Her entire face. A cool feeling swam from her neck to her back. The monstrous sound of dog slobber dimmed to a regular volume. She reached up to push Jada away. Ryan whistled. And then Jada was gone. "Talk to me Teagan." She heard him pour the liquid again. "What movie did you ladies watch last week?"

Last week? Only a week had gone by?

"I don't think I can remember."

"Try. We had practise after school. Do you remember that?" The scent of the food beckoned to her. She stared at her lap, then shook her head. He sat back and held a thermos in his hand. From the overhead light, the goosebumps prickling his arms were visible.

Now you know how it feels to be down here! The thought didn't help with her current misery. Her eyes were suddenly heavy and warm.

202

"Hey!" She heard him first. Then saw his arm stretched out to her foot. A hand ran up and down her back. Annie's hand. "You told me you and Annie were going out that evening. You said your movie was at 8:30."

"You picked us up." She suddenly recalled. She straightened her back. "We were... waiting... and then walking... and then there were lights..." The memories were short flashes of images. "You were mad... said we shouldn't have been out that late..." She could picture his silhouette approaching them in the glow from the headlights. "You told us... you'd drive us home..." She stopped, and looked up at him. "You knew we'd be at the theatre. You planned this!"

He put the lid back on the thermos. "Yeah. That's why I was there." He set it down and lifted a small bottle, which he started to shake. She diverted her gaze and stared straight ahead.

"At practise that day... you knew..." Her voice rose. Then cracked. "You... you coached us... talked to us as part of your team... but you - you..." A tear slipped down her cheek.

"Teagan..." He looked down. "Nothing I say can change what I did." He paused. "What I've done." He rubbed the back of his neck. "But, I'm sorry. I would change things if I could. That's not enough; I know that. And you can stay angry with me for as long as you want." He set his jaw, then redirected his gaze to Annie. "This is cold medicine." He poured it onto a spoon and lifted it to Annie's mouth. "How's your temperature doing?" He pressed his hand pressed against Annie's forehead.

203

"But why us? What did we do to make you do this to us?" Teagan's voice was louder than before.

"Shhh, I'll tell you everything as soon as you're well enough to understand." He took the spoon back out of Annie's mouth. His words didn't calm her though. Not at all. And he was ignoring her questions by talking to Annie! "Annie, come back here, so you can lean against the wall. Bring the sleeping bag too." His hand was on Teagan's shoulder, holding her up.

"It's okay, Teagan." Annie said quietly. She moved away and took the blanket with her.

"Why is this happening?" She cried. "Annie! Why are you letting him tell you what to do?"

Annie turned back with a startled expression. "It's okay, Teagan." She repeated and nodded once to reassure her. Jada began to lick Teagan's face again. She tried to pull away and push Jada away.

Ryan spoke to Annie again. "There is good. I'm going to move Teagan to sit in front of you, okay? Jada, go." He easily slid Teagan in front of Annie and Annie wrapped her arms around her from behind. Ryan tugged the blanket tightly around both of them, then looked past her and continued to ignore her burning questions. "Annie, how are you feeling? Have your insides warmed up a bit?"

"I think so. Thanks." Her voice was soft. And tired. She breathed on Teagan's ear with each word.

"Okay, you can sleep for a bit if you want. You'll be alright. In about an hour I'll get some steam going in the bathroom and if you feel

204

strong enough, you can shower. How does that sound? We just need to wait a bit so you two don't go into shock, okay?" He settled back in front of Teagan and picked up the thermos. He whistled again and seconds later, Jada was back sitting on top of her lap.

"Ryan! You didn't answer my questions!" Teagan wiped tears from her face. He poured out the delicious smelling contents. The steam rose and touched her skin. He squared his gaze with hers and he lifted a cup.

"Listen, I need you to focus on warming up, alright? I'll answer all your questions later. I promise. Let's get some food into you." Teagan twisted her lips. He'd sidestepped her questions again. Maybe he'd never tell her. He tilted his head, the way he did when he was about to get mad.

"How do I know you didn't put drugs in there to make me pass out and forget this conversation?" She demanded.

He narrowed his eyes. "You don't."

"Well, I'm not hungry then." She crossed her arms. And then remembered that he couldn't see them beneath the blanket.

"Really, Teagan?" He sighed. "I'm trying to help you feel better."

"For what? So you can torture us again?" She nearly shouted. He put down the thermos and cup.

"Do you want to change your tone and restart this conversation? Because I'm not talking to you like this."

She pursed her lips and scowled. "I said, '*I'm not hungry.*'"

"And this isn't an offer."

"But I don't trust you!" She shouted.

"That's fine. I don't deserve to have your trust after what I've done. But if you don't take this, you'll die right here, in front of me. No more friends, no more boys. And no more soccer."

She rolled her eyes to try and show that none of that mattered. But really, those were the most important things to her. "I can't have any of that stuff down here anyway."

"I know, and I'm sorry. But things are going to get better soon. I can't make it up to you right away, but I promise I'll try."

She wet her lips and as she did, her stomach groaned. All three of them heard it. "How will things get better?"

"Food first. Then medicine. And then we'll talk."

She studied his eyes for a moment, searching for anger or fakery. He raised his eyebrows and waited. He looked exhausted and she couldn't decide if that was a good thing or not. "I'll have some, I guess." She watched as he nodded and poured contents into the cup. After about fifteen minutes, he gave her cold medicine to help with her symptoms. And she fell asleep soon after that.

J. M. Bergman

Chapter 15

10:45 AM

Jeffrey Spade strolled through the train station with his briefcase in tow. A fresh, crew-cut hairstyle polished his professional look. He wore a black suit and tie, carried a large cardboard coffee cup and had donned glasses as an extra attempt to look like the businessman he professed to be. Smells of various cigarettes and engine oils filled the air.

He and Ryan went way back. They'd met in their early twenties right before Jeff hit a rough patch. A suicidal, drug addicted rough patch that would have killed him if it hadn't been for Ryan's support. His own family had sworn him off and said he'd never make anything out of himself. But Ryan didn't give up on him. He stood beside him until he became clean. No questions asked. So when Ryan approached him several weeks ago with a dangerous plan involving police and money, he hadn't hesitated. Nor did he ask for more information than what was given. And aside from backing up Ryan's alibi a few days ago, Jeff hadn't done anything illegal yet.

He joined a crowd around a suspended flat screen TV and gazed to a nearby metal bench where the 'package' was set to be delivered. He glanced at his watch: 10:57 AM. A candied fragrance passed by, and a young woman with a giggling child walked past. They meandered forward and she sat on the bench. The toddler jumped on the seat and peered back toward him. Blonde hair curled around a mischievous face.

Let's see what happens, he thought.

A tall, stocky-looking gentleman approached the bench from a different direction, with a briefcase. His black shoes echoed off the tiled floor and he wore a beige trench coat. He sat down at the other side of the bench. Jeff waited. Signals would be difficult to pass with civilians interfering. He sipped at his coffee; one sugar, three creams - so bad, but so good at the same time. He glanced at his watch again: 10:59 AM.

The child began to hop and scream on the bench. The flustered mother, who appeared more concerned with her cell phone, lifted him and went for the vending machine. Mr. Trenchcoat lay the briefcase on the bench beside him. He placed his brown hat on the case, palmed the back of his neck and made the peace sign with his fingers.

There it was. The signal Jeff had waited for.

He glanced at the arrival and departure times on the screen once more for appearance, then made his way to the bench. A policeman stalked across the platform. Jeff stopped and turned away from the cop.

He knew police were involved, but Ryan had been clear that they shouldn't be interfering today. He made a mental note to ditch the suit jacket and glasses once he got on the train.

A wall clock read: 11:02 AM now. He stole a glance over his shoulder. The cop had continued around the perimeter of the station. Thundering sounds of an approaching train came into earshot. He took a nervous breath. Jeff chewed his lip. He had three minutes to get this done and make his escape.

If this goes sour... No. He owed it to Ryan.

He readjusted the fake glasses and made his way to the bench. He took a seat, and nonchalantly greeted the stranger. "We have some business to discuss", he said, quoting the cue Ryan had given him.

"It starts with the message." The man replied, keeping his gaze ahead. Perfect exchange. Word for word.

"Everything you need to know is in here." Jeff took a sealed envelope out of his suit pocket and handed it sideways, also keeping his gaze ahead. Ryan had let him read the contents and instructed him how to respond in the event of questions.

Release Time - 2:00 PM

Central Train Station

No police

If anyone follows after the ransom delivery, one hostage will be shot.

The man opened the envelope and studied the words while Jeff cracked the man's briefcase. Then he stood. "We're good?" He still didn't look down at Jeff.

"We're good." Jeff replied. The man put the envelope in his pocket and walked away.

Well, that wasn't so bad, Jeff thought to himself. He opened his own briefcase and slid the smaller one inside. He snapped the clasps to close it and hurried to join the boarding line for the train. Still no trouble from that cop. If everything went according to plan, Jeff wouldn't have the briefcase for long anyway, even if someone did follow him. But he wanted a better explanation from Ryan later about his back-up plan concerning the message he just handed out. Because Ryan wouldn't shoot a hostage. No way. He did however have a way of convincing people that he'd do as he said.

Jeff stepped onto the train. He pocketed the glasses, then started down the aisle, keeping his eyes sharp for his target. The scents of coffee, sweat and fast food filled the area around him. "Excuse me", he said, turning sideways to allow an older gentleman to pass. He slipped the suit coat off and draped it over the briefcase handle in his hand. He turned his head a couple times, and looked over his shoulder. He saw a flash of auburn hair down the aisle ahead of him. Samantha, or 'Sam', his beautiful girlfriend. She looked professional as well and had an identical briefcase in tow. He refused to allow his face to show recognition of her in case someone caught the exchange. They were five feet apart when he faked a trip and stumbled forward.

"Oh, no!" He gasped, pulling his briefcase to the front to catch his fall. His coat covered both handles. She stepped sideways and cast an irritated glance. "Sorry", he mumbled, and let go of the case and took hers. He watched her take the handle of his, then they continued down the aisle in the opposite directions.

***

Sam stepped off the train and pulled out a pair of shades. She walked briskly through the station, trying to blend into the crowd that had exited with her. Sounds of high heel shoes and a crying baby mixed with her thoughts as she stepped into the station building itself. Her own high heels now echoed off the walls of candy dispensers. Finally, she pushed through the exit door and out onto the cool street corner.

Almost done. She grinned and mentally patted herself on the back for getting this far without any problems. She and Jeff had pulled cons for years. It made for a life of adventure, danger and mystery, with new identities every so often. And that was where she thrived. She hailed a taxi and pushed her blowing brown hair behind her ears.

"Burlingham Drive, please." She slid inside.

"Would you like me to take your bag, ma'am?"

"No, it's alright, thank you." She folded the handle into the briefcase, set it by her feet, and began to pull the door closed, but a man with blonde dreads, a bandana and green army bag grabbed the door and peeked inside.

"Hey, lovely." He grinned and winked. "Mind if I share this ride?"

"Um, sure." She cleared her throat, as if working up the nerve to share a ride with an unknown male. But it was Jeff's cousin, Freddie. She slid over for him to squeeze in. Truth was, they spent a lot of time together. Ryan's last minute request to include him was hilarious. But then again, how many people could you trust with picking up a ransom?

"Your bag, sir?" The cabbie questioned.

"Thanks, brother, but I like to hold onto my goods." A long tye-dyed shirt and baggy pants covered his pale skin. He looked like a homeless musician, and that was without planning a disguise.

"Where to, sir?"

"Oh, just Wynters, brother." A few blocks from here. Sam knew that Freddie would get out there and then hail another cab which would take him to Ryan's. He unzipped his bag that sat at his feet. "Now where are my running shoes?" He acted as though he were rifling through the contents, while really he tucked Sam's briefcase inside. Then pulled out a different one for her to carry. "Ah, here we are."

She watched as he pulled out Adidas runners (Ryan's runners. Freddie didn't exercise. At all.), and put his flip flops into the bag. Yes, he still wore them in this frosty weather. She watched him slide on the runners and 'coughed' to divert her laughter, because Freddie's feet swam in the shoes. The runners hadn't even been part of the plan, but

213

when Freddie had gone over to Ryan's earlier to check for the key, he'd also let himself in and decided he wanted to add something to his 'undercover' character too.

Apparently, he hadn't tried them on.

"This is me, brother." He waved at the driver in the rear-view mirror, and handed a five-dollar bill forward. "Keep the change."

Samantha allowed herself to glance back his way as he stepped out. He nearly tripped on the curb because the shoes were longer than his own feet. He caught himself and turned back to smile at the driver and wave good-bye.

J. M. Bergman

Chapter 16

The empty thermoses sat on the cement floor near both sleeping girls. A few hours had passed since they'd spoken last. In the entrance Ryan wore the second sweater he'd packed for himself and chased Jada around the staircase to keep warm and burn off steam. Between checking the girls every quarter hour and worrying about the ransom drop, he'd nearly dug a path through the concrete. His watch beeped again as Jada rushed past. He bent down and caught her head and kissed her between the ears. Then went back into back to the cell. Teagan lifted her head and looked up at him.

"How you feeling?" He crouched down to her eye level.

"Fine, I guess." Sleeping hadn't helped with her anger toward him.

"Let me check your pulse." He held his hand open, waiting. She looked like she was deciding whether it was worth putting up a fight or not. But a moment later she put out her wrist for him to take. She didn't want to look at him. And that was okay. It would have to be. He of all people knew the fragility of trust. That it needed to be earned. And also could be lost. Her body temperature had risen. He let his gaze wander while his thumb felt her heart rate. Her pulse was much better. He twisted his hand so that his own wrist sat in her palm.

"Squeeze."

"Why?" She frowned.

"To check if your strength is back."

"Oh." She stared blankly, then tightened her grip.

"Harder", he encouraged. "Hold it, hold it. Okay, good." He pulled his hand away. She was still weaker than usual. His stitches felt like piercing needles from the cold and his biceps ached beneath them. He winced, and noticed Teagan watching him curiously. "I'm really sorry." He balled his fists and blew warmth into them. "I honestly had no idea it would get this cold down here."

A stubborn look flashed across her face for a second, but he saw her bite back her thoughts. "Thanks for the food and stuff."

"Yeah." He noticed Annie had opened her eyes too. "Annie, let me check your pulse. How do you feel?"

She held out her wrist. "I'm still cold, Ryan."

"I'm sorry." He whispered and held her stare for a moment. "Let's get some more medicine into you both." He reached into his backpack and withdrew the small bottle again, along with the two spoons he'd brought. Annie took her medicine and thanked him, but Teagan put up another little fight. Ryan decided not to argue this time,

217

and eventually she took her medicine too. "I'll get steam going in the bathroom, then we can go sit in there where it's warm, alright?" He waited for them to nod, then rose and crossed the room. Once inside, the tropical smell of female shampoo filled the air. Shampoo and soap he'd left here for the girls sat in bottles on the floor. He pulled the shower on and hovered near the hot water as steam lifted and clung to his skin. He turned the sink water to hot as well, then went back for his guests. He stopped short.

Teagan stood in the center of the room with his knife extended from her shaking hand. She looked like a viper, prepared to attack. Her eyes were filled with dangerous emotions. Annie stood apprehensively, a couple feet behind.

Ryan spread his palms open at his sides, as he had done with Wade, and spoke in a steady tone. "What's going on, Teagan?"

"Let us go." She hissed. He tilted his head and took a step forward. "Stop! Or I swear I'll run this into your heart!"

"Teagan, don't do this." Another step.

She curled her lips into a snarl. "Give me one good reason! After all the pain you've caused us - you deserve to die!"

"You're mad at me. And that's fair." He stopped in front of her, feet shoulder width apart. "You don't understand what -"

"Then make me understand!" She screamed. Annie flinched.

"Teagan, put the knife down. Now." His tone hardened. "You know I'm stronger than you. I don't want you to get hurt."

"You already hurt me! You hurt us both!" She bared her teeth. "Tell me why you took us!"

Ryan swallowed and pressed his lips together. "I will. But first you need to drop the knife." She started to shift her weight between her legs. She'd unleash any moment. "Listen, there are people who want to hurt you..." He glanced at the weapon, then back at her eyes. "Both of you. I brought you here to protect you."

"LIAR!" She lunged for his gut, but in one motion he dropped his arms and grabbed the side of her wrist, spinning her body away. He wrapped his other arm around her and held her hands together. "AHH!" She screamed, squirming in his grasp. "You're a filthy animal! I hate you!"

"Let go of the knife." He said between his teeth as she squirmed. The top of her head bobbed inches from his face.

"No!" She twisted her weak body and tried to elbow his chest.

"Teagan! I'm only going to ask you one more time: Drop it." It would be easy to force his command, but forcing her to do anything at this point wouldn't help with his apology. She snapped her head back and he barely dodged getting hit in the face. He put pressure on her wrists with his thumbs. *Come on, just back down...* She started to kick back against his shin. "Hey -" *Okay, this ends now.* He twisted her wrists fast.

"Ah!" she gasped. The knife fell and crashed against the floor. He kept her hands together, but loosened his grip. Her heavy breathing was the only sound they heard in the following silence as he waited and

219

tried to move past her stubborn aggression. Any other time, anger would have taken over his actions already, but not today. It was time for his inappropriate behaviour to change. He met Annie's scared eyes as Teagan's body began to shake. Her breathing turned jagged and she began to sob. He closed his eyes. No more mind games. They needed to know the truth.

He took a breath. "Annie we're here because of your family. If you want it straight, I'll tell you, but it'll hurt. Your call."

Annie's eyes filled with confusion and stepped forward. "My family? You don't even know my family, Ryan. What are you talking about?"

"It's complicated. I can give you the basics today if you want, and then once you get over that I can tell you more."

"I just... don't understand." She stared up at him with a blank expression, but her eyes began to harden with courage. He hated that he was about to break her again. "Don't you dare lie to me." She clenched her fists at her side, and he began to wonder if he'd have to take her down too.

"No lies. I promise."

"Okay. Tell me everything."

"Are you sure?"

She nodded once.

"Okay, here goes: A pregnant patient died nine years ago after taking a drug your dad had introduced. The medicine was supposed to help her baby, but it killed both of them." He stopped and watched her

220

react. It would be hard news for anyone to hear and it looked like a sucker-punch to her gentle nature. "Do you want me to keep going?"

"What? There's more?" She crossed her arms. A defense mechanism he'd used many times himself.

"Yeah." He couldn't decide whether to water down the details or just lay out the facts. His throat had become dry.

"Okay. How does this involve me and Teagan?"

"The patient's husband is…" He swallowed and tried for the hundredth time to think of a way to soften the coming blow. "The patient's husband is your uncle." The words hit her hard and she stumbled backwards into the wall. A ghostly expression settled over her eyes. Ryan looked away for a moment, then whispered, "I'm sorry. He wanted revenge…and decided to kill the people your dad loved. Starting with your mom."

Annie's fingers shook and spread out against the cold wall. Her whole body was shaking.

"I brought you here because -" He paused. "He wants you and Teagan dead too. He told me -" He sighed. "He manipulated me into taking you. I was his puppet, because - of something I did a long time ago. He said you could live if I tortured you. That's why I used the drugs…so it wouldn't hurt as much." He tried to sound confident, like the hero he thought he would be, but even as he said it, self-loathing crawled through him.

I took you because I couldn't man up and take the consequences of my actions.

221

No one spoke. Annie's face had turned white. He knew that look. Had worn it several times himself. Her legs collapsed and she slid down the wall. She stared straight ahead. She'd close up now, just like he had feared. Block out the world. Block out the pain like he had done as a child, before choosing to fight back.

"Hey, can you still hear me?" Maybe he could still save her. Pull her out before she slipped away. Teagan's weight suddenly anchored on his arm. The stitches groaned and he gasped. "Ah! Hey, Teagan, stand up. Teagan?" She didn't respond.
He glanced back at Annie.

One girl at a time.

He sighed and hobbled to the washroom with Teagan draped over his good arm. Steam extended toward them and he lowered her to the floor against a wall, then knelt in front of her. Her head hung to one side. He reached for her face to take a look at her pupils, but then drew back. This was a familiar situation. And as much as he wanted to help her, he didn't trust her. He tapped her shoulder a few times. Then tried waving his hand in front of her eyes. Still nothing. He let out a long breath, then covered his nose to keep it safe, and leaned in to pry an eyelid open. She jumped and came to, blinking several times. She looked up at the light first, then sideways to the shower and finally at him.

"Hey. You okay?" He continued to watch her eyes adjust while he took her wrist for another pulse check.

"Where are we?"

222

"The bathroom. Annie's in the other room." Her heart rate was a bit stronger. She looked as though she were studying his face, then she gazed around the bathroom again. "Are you okay?" He repeated.

"I had a dream that I stole your knife." She stared at him and brushed her hair away from her face. Then did a double-take at her unbound wrist.

"Oh yeah? What happened?" He flipped her hand to hold his wrist. "Squeeze."

"Why are we in the bathroom?" She pushed away from the wall and started to look side to side. "Where's Annie?" She noticed his wrist in her hand and dropped it. "Where's Annie?"

"Teagan, it's okay. You're okay. Annie is in the other room with Jada."

She started to hyperventilate. "Did I do something wrong? Did you hurt Annie again because of me?" She whipped her head back and forth and began to gasp and cry. "Annie? Annie!" He took hold of her wrists.

"Teagan, look at me - hey, look at me." She did as tears streaked down her cheeks. "It's okay. Nothing bad is going to happen to you or Annie."

"My dream... was it real?" She whispered. "Did I steal your knife?"

He held her gaze. "It's okay, Teagan. It's okay."

She let her head fall back against the wall and closed her eyes as she cried. "I'm sorry... I'm sorry... please, don't hurt Annie…"

He dropped her wrists and stood to get her a bottle of water. "Teagan, can you drink this? It's just water, I promise." Her face was scrunched up with emotion and she considered him for a few seconds, but then reached for the bottle. He let her put her hand around it, but also held on as she brought it to her mouth and drank. After about a minute she let go and he set it beside her. "You don't have to be scared of me anymore, Teagan. I'll never hurt you again."

"Why are you doing this?" She sniffed and wiped her nose. "You're trying to trick me."

He dropped his chin to his chest. "No, I'm not." He looked back up to her. "Listen, I messed up. Big time. This never should have happened." He explained the situation again while she stared back at him with hurt, untrusting eyes. If his younger self were only here to see what a mess he'd made… His lips began to tremble, even though he tried to make them stop. "I owe you both the world for this."

She looked at her lap and her brown bangs fell over her eyes. He took the moment to steady his breathing. Her short hair reminded him of how badly he'd failed. "Thanks for not killing us…I guess", she muttered. She fingered a loose thread on her jeans. Small white cracks from the cold air lined her hands. "Why didn't you tell us?" Her hazel eyes were still wet. "Instead of all this?"

He opened his mouth to respond, but closed it, because he didn't have a legitimate excuse. "I'd redo everything if I could." Still so many things she wouldn't understand. She sniffed an unsteady breath and looked away. "I took that picture after I cut your hair to prove you were suffering down here. It was part of the deal." He bit his lip as she looked back up at him. She may as well have ripped his heart out with her sad eyes.

After a moment, she looked away again. "I get it."

"Hey, what would make this better? Right now, if you could have anything." His brown eyes searched her face.

Really? As if anything you do could make her feel better. He shook away the thoughts and looked at the floor.

"I don't know. Is Annie okay?" She stared at her lap again, having none of it. That's fair if he had to work for it.

"Tell you what: I'm going to close my eyes, and you -" He lifted her baggy-sweatered arm. "You're going to punch me as hard as you can." A playful light flickered behind her eyes, then died. "Really. Anywhere you want." He curled his lips into a partial grin, then became serious again and he closed his eyes.

"What?"

He peeked through one eye. "I'm serious. You know you want to." His eye closed again and he waited.

"Um, okay..." She said, in a tone much too shy for her, and lightly punched his shoulder.

"Ow!" He gasped and shot his arm up to rub the spot. "Ow..." He grunted and shook his shoulders.

"That didn't even hurt!" She cried out.

"Are you kidding?" He complained, faking deep pain. He shook out his shoulders again, cleared his throat, then closed his eyes and

225

nodded. "Okay, give it to me. Everything you've got." Her fist drove into his gut this time, which forced a legitimate cringe. He multiplied the reaction.

"Ahh!" He groaned, scrunching his face and nursing his side with his hand. He stared at her with deep hurt. That got him a small giggle. "Okay. One more. Make it count." He coached. The room went silent. Neither of them moved. "Okay, you're killing me here", He quipped seriously from behind closed eyes. He heard a quick inhale and she struck his sore jaw, nearly tipping him backward from the force. "Aww!" He massaged the skin and looked to the floor to regain his bearings. Maybe there should have been rules to this game. When he glanced up, she was watching him timidly. "That one's on me." He cast a grin and shook his head. Then he held out his fist, just like he would before sending her onto the field. She sucked in a breath. This was a gesture from their life before...when he was her friend. A smile snuck through her eyes. She punched back, and their hands mimicked each other through a series of bunts, which ended with a high five. Then he pushed up off his knees and stood. "We can do this again later if you want." He winked and headed back out.

Annie hadn't moved from the wall. Her lopsided legs lay haphazardly on the floor.

"Hey, Jeffreys." Looking at her tear-streaked face brought more pain in his chest than he could have imagined. Another lost child. Not just separated from a family. Her world had been taken away. "Annie…" He crouched on his knee. "None of this is your fault. You haven't done anything wrong. It's an adult war. You and Teagan are victims." She still wouldn't acknowledge him. He sighed, "I'm sincerely sorry for what happened to your mom. It's terrible."

"How long have you known?" Her dark eyes stared past him and he hesitated. "Tell me."

"Annie, this -"

"How long?"

His mouth remained parted from the previous words. He cleared his throat. "A few months." He could see her mind doing the math behind her eyes.

"So before school even started... before the season..." She gaped. "You knew this whole time that you would take us?" Her eyes glittered. Everything inside pushed him to look away. To get up and walk away and wait until the emotions passed. To fold up like a coward. But not today. The least he could do was look her in the eyes and face the consequences of her tears head on.

"Yeah, I knew."

And every time I saw you two on the field I tried to think of a way to save you!

She bit her lip and looked away as another tear escaped.

He took a breath. "It killed me to know what was going on behind the scenes. I -" He hesitated. "I brought you here to protect you. You were supposed to be safe here." His face flushed and burned from his shame. He tried to clear the dry knot from his throat. "I failed." He shook his head. And then had to break his gaze. How on earth had he let his behaviour get so out of hand? "I'm a bad person, Annie."

"But you said you were the good guy."

"That's what I thought." He tried desperately to clear his throat again. "I was wrong." That wasn't good enough for an apology. But it was a start. "Do you understand why I couldn't let you escape?"

She looked away. "I guess."

"I thought that... if I scared you enough you'd listen to me and stay here. Look, I feel like a complete idiot."

"I've always listened to you, Ryan! I would have done anything you asked!" Her voice cracked and she broke into a sob.

"I know." He glanced up from beneath his eyebrows, but the coward in him took over and he had to look away. "I should have done things way differently."

"Yes, you should have!" She punched below his sternum, hard. He gasped and blinked at the ground.

Don't get mad, don't get mad. Remember, you taught her how to defend herself.

He licked his lips and met her eyes. "I deserved that."

"You deserve way more than that! You almost killed us, Ryan! And you drugged us! Drugs! We could be messed up forever now because of you!" She hit his arm, and he took the hit. Tears trickled down her cheeks. "And you - you cut my skin!" She hit him again and again as she cried. He forced himself to hold her gaze as her face turned red, and to take whatever she threw at him. To accept that he was

228

responsible for this lost child's pain. He blinked several times as he recalled images of the knife cutting through her skin. Of her screaming beneath his grasp in the woods. Tears began to pool in his eyes.

"Annie, what I did to you and Teagan was criminal." He shook his head. "I can't erase it, but I'm sorry. I'll do anything you want to make it up to you. To start making it up to you", he corrected. There was more truth to tell her. But she wouldn't be able to handle it. Not yet. She frowned. "You can stay angry at me for the rest of your life if you want." His chest weighed like cement. "Remember when you said you 'wished I choked on my own blood'?" Her pupils dilated in fear. "I deserved that too."

Her lips pressed together. "I told you that I didn't mean what I said."

"Oh, I'm pretty sure you did!" He scoffed, remembering her unleashed anger. She blushed and looked down. "I violated your trust, and I wish I could take back what I did. I know you have questions and things you want to say to me." He erased anger and remorse from his face, to try and show he was open. "Let's hash this out. Right here. What else do you have to say to me?"

Her dark hair hung in layers over the green sweater. After a moment, she spoke. "That..." She searched his eyes for aggression. "It's not fair."

"You're right. What else?" He blinked to kill the tears from a moment ago. The light above flickered.

229

"You betrayed us and you shouldn't be coaching our team." Her voice gained confidence. "And I wish I could make you feel our pain... I wish I could lock you down here and make you freeze and starve!" She breathed heavily.

"You'd like that, huh? Maybe we can work something out." He winked. "I know that I owe you way more than an apology. But that's all I've got right now. I'm sorry. I'm really sorry."

She fingered through a strand of hair. Then bit her lip.

"I can start doing push-ups if that'll make you feel any better." He offered a sheepish half-grin, but she narrowed her eyes at him and looked away. Tough kid to crack. "Hey, you remember my scars?" He shrugged the arm she had noticed earlier. "A taste of my own medicine, don't you think?" She blinked up at him, expressionless. Not having any of it. He sighed, "I honestly don't know what the future looks like, but I can bring you whatever you want for down here, alright? Or we can leave. Go some place fun if you want."

"Why can't you tell the police about the family who killed my mom?" She interjected. "So, we can go home."

He drew in a jagged breath. "Because -" He scratched the back of his neck. "Because it's not that simple."

Her shoulders fell. "Of course, it's not."

They sat in silence for a moment. "Hey, you wanna know what made me realize I need to change?"

"What?" He noticed a braid forming beneath her fingers

"The God Cadence talks about." The hair dropped from her hands and her eyes widened. He suddenly felt self-conscious and his eyes wandered to the floor. "Can you believe that?"

"Of course, I can." She dropped the braid and stared up at him.

"What? You're not going to run me into the ground about my beliefs the way I did to you?"

"What good would that do? I told you he could see us."

"Yeah. You did say that."

"I know he can." Her brown eyes shone with conviction and she jabbed her finger through the air. "I know something bad happened to you, Ryan. And I knew that way before you were planning to kidnap us!"

He narrowed his eyes. "'Team Annie' takes the lead on the scoreboard." He punched her knee when she rolled her eyes. "I'm kidding." He grew serious. "You're right. You and Cadence. You two could make a living off your intuition."

"It's more than intuition, Ryan."

Yeah, he knew that, too. The voice that knew his past. The one who protected him from a killer. The one who showed him how to change. He still couldn't pinpoint what the voice wanted with him though.

"Alright, Jeffreys..." Her eyes filled with expectancy. "Look, I can't tell you everything now. But you're right. Something bad happened. A long time ago. But how about we get through this abduction thing first?"

"Fine." She looked away and began to pull her hands through her hair again. "Where's Teagan?"

He chewed at the inside of his mouth. Today was the first time he'd ever initiated a discussion about religion - and he just had the feeling that there was more to it that he didn't know yet. "What else do you know about Him, Annie?"

"About whom?"

He groaned and felt his pride diminish. *Don't make me beg!* "God...I think."

"You want to bring *God* into this?" She quoted him and smirked. He clenched his jaw, looked to the ceiling, then to the floor. There it was. The jab he'd been anticipating. But it came after he'd opened up to her. He was already at her mercy for forgiveness, and then he'd gone and stepped one platform lower. Nice play on her part. He rubbed his forehead while shaking his head.

"What else do you want to know?" Her eyes glinted in the dim light.

"Forget it." He pushed up off his knees and started to stand.

"Hey!" She shouted.

He scrunched his brows and stopped halfway up.

"Sit down!"

"Excuse me?"

"You asked me a question and now you're going to listen to me answer it! Sit down, Grey!" She pointed at the floor.

He felt his mouth part. "Yes, ma'am." He crouched down and she squirmed in her seat and adjusted to sit up on her knees so they were eye to eye.

Wow, the day he thought he'd be unnerved by Annie...

"God not only sees everything, Ryan - He created this entire universe with words and thought you and I were important enough to be included in it! Your life is a miracle. My life is a miracle!" She pointed at him then herself. "We're not an accident, Ryan. He brought us to this exact moment! Whatever happened to you wasn't right, but you don't have to let that drag you down for the rest of your life. You can be free! Jesus can set you free!"

He pulled his chin back to avoid her flailing hand. Her eyes had ignited and her sweater sleeves swung with her movements. He started to anticipate another fist fight and knocked her hand away. "Take a breath -"

"You're more than just a man, Ryan. More than a coach. You're his child. I'm his child! He cares about us! He sees us! My mom was killed and now I've been abducted - but He's still the king! If it's my time to go home to Him, then it's my time. But my time hasn't come yet and neither has yours!"

"Preach it, girl!" Teagan chimed from the bathroom door. Ryan glanced back and saw her peek out of the bathroom mischievously. "Annie, drop the mic and walk away. You should come in here with me, it's way warmer."

He returned his gaze to Annie, who now stood on her knees and stared intently into his eyes, less than a foot away from his face. "Wow... uh, well, you definitely know how to deliver." He scratched the back of his head and stared at her in amusement. "Not sure how to follow that."

"Well, I tried to tell you before." She sat back down. *Yeah, she did.* The day he shut down her encouragement and took away her breakfast.

"Why do you care if I believe all this or not?" He suddenly wondered out loud.

"Because he wants you to know the truth, or else he wouldn't have told me to tell you." A stubborn serenity crossed her face.

"You're giving me *his* message? After everything I've done to you?" He challenged. "Why would you do that?"

She pressed her lips together. "Because I know who I am. And I'll do whatever He asks." She swept her hair over her shoulder.

"Oh, I see. Did He tell you to yell at me like that, too?" Annie laughed and tucked the sweater around her. A clean feeling washed over Ryan's chest as her words sunk in. She cared about him as a person. As someone who mattered. A friend. Not a criminal. She saw him outside of his crimes. About half an hour later he told them he had to leave to finish up some business, but that he'd be back soon. He took orders for dinner: pizza, chicken wings and chocolate cake, then headed back up the stairs.

J. M. Bergman

But the three of them would never be together in the bunker again.

Chapter 17

Ryan dashed up his cedar steps and pushed the front door open. The end of his crazy involvement with this family was in sight. The money would be split up and he'd call the relationship with Michelle off. He'd left his supplies at the bunker with instructions to shower, relax, and stay underground. The environment was still hostile for them and they had to stay hidden.

"The hatch will be covered with a heavy, dead tree." He'd told them. "I do that everyday to keep it hidden. You two stay together downstairs and take care of each other." He'd left Jada behind as well to keep them warm.

Now he ran to the locked safe in his bedroom closet. His clothes hung in front of a stack of boxes, which he lifted away and the grey box sat before him. Twisting the safe dial to six special numbers led to a satisfying, 'click'. He held his breath, then slowly pulled the door open. The briefcase sat before him. He took a breath and gingerly opened it, and what he saw caused a wave of long-anticipated satisfaction. Cold cash. The plan had worked. It was as if heavy sandbags on his shoulders had dissolved into thin air. He finally exhaled.

"So, it's all there?" He nearly jumped, and spun to face the voice. Michelle stood smiling behind him. He deliberately sighed loudly and rolled his eyes.

"You scared me." He stood and turned to face her. She laughed smoothly.

"We did it!" She shrieked, opening her arms for his embrace. Her charismatic turquoise eyes were irresistible to turn from. They sparkled like a refreshing brook. He allowed himself a moment of indulgence and accepted her into his arms.

"Yeah, we pulled it off." The scent of fresh rain rose from her hair and swam around his face.

"Let's celebrate!" She grabbed his hand and led him to the living room. "I brought champagne!" Suddenly her body was pressing against his and her lips were working their magic. Before he even realized what happened, she had pulled away. Breathtaking. He stood, stunned by her craft. His blood pumped a million miles a minute, begging him to follow her. To forget about her part in all this. Her happiness somehow made him feel like a bigger man.

He heard a vehicle door slam in front of the house. Who could that be? The mission was over. Finished. Nobody else needed to be involved. He peeked out the front window and his legs grew numb.

***

Officer Banks walked up the stairs to Ryan Grey's home. The Fischer and Jeffreys girls still had not been released as promised and now it was time to pry further into their contacts to search for the kidnappers. Rachel Fischer had told him that Teagan practically lived on the soccer field, and only came home to eat and sleep. And that Teagan would often try and skip family events because her coach was offering an extra soccer clinic or fitness boot camp. Lydia Jeffreys had similar things to say about Annie. So, either these girls were close to their coach or they legitimately loved soccer above everything else.

He rapped at the entrance, and about half a minute later, the door opened. Ryan Grey stood well over six feet tall. His lean body showed muscle in his arms and chest. He was dressed in a black t-shirt and track pants and looked like he'd just gotten home from doing something physical.

"Can I help you?" He asked, after the initial shock of having a police officer at his door had passed.

"Officer Banks." He stated, extending his hand. They shook. "I'm here about Teagan Fischer and Annie Jeffreys. Have a minute for a few questions?"

"Absolutely." Ryan stepped onto his porch and shut the door behind him. He furrowed his eyebrows and crossed his arms. "Still no sign of them?"

"Unfortunately, not. When was the last time you saw either of them?"

"We had a game Saturday afternoon. Uh, they both played well."

Banks nodded and jotted down the information. "Did they mention any plans to you? Anything about a weekend trip away from home?"

"Not at all. Just that they were going to see a movie together that evening." He shook his head. "The team had practise the next morning and I was shocked when they didn't show. Nationals are in three weeks and they both know they'd be benched for skipping."

"I see." Officer Banks scratched his ear. "You do realize that as their coach, and apparently one of the people they spend most of their time with, you come up as one of the first suspects in their disappearance."

Ryan blinked and raised his eyebrows. "Oh, well, you can ask anything you want. I'm an open book."

Banks studied him a moment, then flipped to a new page in his notebook. "Where were you Saturday night?"

"I was at my buddy's place. Jeffrey Spade."

"What time? And what were the two of you doing?"

"I got there at eight. We played pool. Had a few drinks. His girlfriend came over around 10:30." Ryan searched the ground. "We watched a movie together."

"Jeffrey Spade." Banks noted the name. "Does Jeffrey have a phone number I can have."

"Absolutely." Ryan pulled his cell out of a pocket and rattled off the digits a few seconds later.

Banks wrote it down. "What's his girlfriend's name? How long was she there?"

"Samantha Prees. She and I left around the same time. It was about two in the morning."

"Okay. You have her number?"

"You bet." He scrolled through his contacts again.

"Alright. That's enough for now. I'll verify your information and contact you again if I need to."

"Yes, please don't hesitate. Honestly, if there is anything I can do to help, please let me know."

Banks nodded. "You ever given thought to joining the force, son? I can tell you're in great shape. I believe you'd be a good fit."

"Thank you, officer."

They shook hands again and he headed back to his cruiser.

***

Ryan stepped back inside and ran his hands through his sweaty hair. His heart raced.

"You handled that well." Michelle approached and ran her fingers up his chest. "Like a champ." She took his hand and led him back to the living room. "You relax right here and start thinking about how we can spend our cash." Her cool hands playfully pressed against his chest, then pushed him down onto the couch. She winked and strode off toward the kitchen.

Yeah. He deserved to celebrate. Annie and Teagan were safe and more wealth than he ever imagined was right here in his home. He'd never have to go without a desire again.

Annie and Teagan have desires too.

Yes, they did. On the field, he'd heard small pieces of their dreams for the future. Annie's plans to pursue medicine. Teagan hoping to become a social worker or lawyer - some days a dentist. His eyes darted, reminding him of where he'd just been. They would have no quality of life in the bunker. He tried to clear his throat, but the thought had formed an enormous weight.

He heard Michelle place two wine glasses on the counter. Their eyes met and she flashed her ravishing smile, before turning away to pour their beverage. There wasn't a happy ending to this story. Not for everyone. He chewed on his lower lip and absently massaged the nape of his neck. The only scenario was if he reported Alec and Michelle to the police. And then they would tell everyone what he had done so many years ago. That was the only way Annie and Teagan could ever really be free.

His life or theirs.

Michelle was strutting toward him now, champagne in hand. Her black-sleeved dress clung to her alluring sides and her eyes pulled at his soul. The disheartening thoughts dissipated again for a moment.

"Here's to starting new." She cooed through her lush lips, sending a shudder through his core. She tipped his glass toward him and their fingers touched. Her eyes were destroying him. He wet his lips and drank, reaching for her other hand. Their fingers interlocked, as she closed her eyes and took a sip. He melted into her skin and caressed her hand. She smiled and gently touched the side of his face. His legs felt as though they were turning to butter.

"How do you do that?" He gushed. Her perfume was captivating and in that moment, he felt as though he could stay here forever,

She laughed. "Do what?" She pushed down on his chest. "What's the matter? You seem...tense." Those eyes! But then a flash of Annie's face hit him. He shook his head and tried to focus. Teagan's soft hair thrown to the floor. A spark of clarity broke through her spell with more images of the girl's tears just an hour ago. His expression changed.

"Wait."

She pulled back. "What's going on with you?"

"Look, we need to talk." He frowned, and felt like the stupidest man alive as he swallowed and pushed himself to continue. He moved his hand to her elbow and forced himself to break away from her eyes. "I don't know if I can do this anymore."

"Do what, babe? There isn't anything left to do."

"No, I mean -" His insides beat against his chest. *Your life or theirs.* He propped himself up against the wall of the couch. "Michelle, I mean 'us'."

"Ryan -" She sat back, and pulled her elbow away. "What are you talking about?"

"Look, this has been fun -"

"You think you can break this off?" She spat. There it was. The killer he'd seen in her eyes so many times. Even money couldn't change that about her.

"This isn't who I am." He settled. "I'm a coach. I help people work out. I don't do secret money-making missions like this!" He paused for clarity. The heaviness of the break up was setting in. He took her hand, but she ripped it away. His shoulders fell. "You have what you wanted now."

She stared at him and shook her head. A terrifying coldness glittered in her eyes. "I knew it. Those little brats got to you, didn't they?"

"What are you talking about?" He immediately felt the same irritation toward her as he had last night.

"You think you're so *noble*, don't you? The 'hero'. Well, you won't need to be a hero anymore after today." She stood. Her dark-heeled shoes made her taller than usual. "Because I'm going to finish what I started."

His heart slammed against his chest. "What do you mean? We have the money." He tried to keep his voice even. "Simon won't see Annie again."

She laughed. "Out of sight, out of mind? That's not real revenge, Ryan. You of all people should know that. You didn't really think we'd let them live, did you? Besides, I want to see the look on Simon's face when he sees their bloody bodies."

"Hey!" He tried to jump to his feet to challenge her, but his legs wouldn't move. His mouth dropped open as he looked down and tried to move again. He'd been drugged. "You witch!"

"Is that the best you got, babe?" She sipped at her own champagne. "If it's any consolation, Alec and I enjoyed the pictures you took.

"No! Lydia, this isn't -"

"It's '*Michelle*' to you! Only my husband calls me by my first name!" She snapped, and stepped back from him. "You're just a pathetic delinquent."

"AHH!" He hollered and forced himself to move but he fell to the floor. He pushed up from his elbows and tried to make his legs work.

"When the police find your prints and scars all over them, no one will question that you've murdered people in the past. That you've been preying on young teenage girls for years...gaining their trust, so you can kidnap them." She smirked. "And me? I'll be the supportive wife of a devastated father. And months from now when I leave him, he'll have nothing to his name but the city's condolences. Unless Alec kills him today." She tipped her glass back again.

"No!" He swung at her legs, but she stepped away.

Her laughter poured out like toxic gas. "Aww, look at you, a poor boy trying to be a hero. You'll have to learn to fight in a man's world if you want to make it out alive." She glided back to the kitchen for her purse. "Oh, I almost forgot -" She pulled a gun out of her bag. He tried to swallow and refused to look away from the weapon. If she was going to kill him, he'd watch the bullet come for him.

"You think Alec will let you live? He may be your brother, but he's deranged, and after everything you know -"

"Shut up, child!" She stalked forward, gun extended. "You're a useless piece of nothing, and those girls are going to die, just like every other kid you failed to protect!" She took another step forward. "I'd finish you right here, but I want you to be thinking about your priorities while we kill them. I'll take a picture to send you when you're in prison." She turned and her heels carried her to his room for the briefcase. He could hear her voice on the phone. "I got it. I'll send you directions and meet you there." A moment later his front door closed.

***

Ryan dug his palms into his forehead and screamed. How had he been so foolish? He had to counteract the drug, now! His hands still moved slowly and he dialed the only person he knew who could help.

Keep a level head, his mind warned.

"Simon, I know where they are!" He shouted.

"What? Who is this?"

"Ryan Grey! You need to pick me up at my house now! Lydia is behind this, she's going to -"

"Ryan, calm down, what do you mean, 'you know where they are'?"

He clenched his fists in frustration. "I took them, Simon! I kidnapped your daughter! You need to pick me up, now!"

Silence came through the line. Then, "You kidnapped Annie?"

"Simon, there's no time, Lydia will kill them!"

"What -"

"My lower body is paralyzed, I need you to bring something to help that."

"What on earth, Ryan?" His disbelief carried anger. The confession was sinking in. Ryan hung up and propped himself up on his elbows, then dragged himself to the kitchen. He pulled open his First Aid drawer and jabbed himself in the leg with an EpiPen.

***

Annie and Teagan sat huddled together on the bathroom floor with both sleeping bags wrapped around them. Water dripped from the sink faucet into the otherwise silent room. The steam had stopped when they ran out of hot water about an hour ago. Jada was curled up on top of both of them again and they were comfortable. But Annie's mind throbbed from the painful information Ryan had shared. Her mother had been killed on purpose. So many things she thought she knew about herself didn't make sense anymore. If Teagan hadn't been here to talk with, her body may have closed into itself.

Screech! The sound of the rusty bunker lid opening came from the entrance. Jada's head shot up and she scrambled off their laps to meet Ryan. Hopefully he'd brought the food they'd requested. Bad times always seemed a bit better with good food. Annie rested her head against the wall and took hold of Teagan's hand.

"It'll be okay." Teagan stated, resting her head-on Annie's shoulder.

"I hope so. As long as he doesn't flip out at us again." She knew the possibility was there and had to prepare for it. But she also felt positive about how their last conversation had gone. "Somehow... I think things will be different with him now."

"Hi, girls. You look cozy."

Annie gasped and scrambled to her feet.

"Lydia!" She cried. Teagan slowly got to her feet. "I can't believe you're here! How did you find us?" Tears began to pool in her eyes. She'd never been so happy to see this woman in her life.

"I know a lot of things, love." She said smoothly and took another step into the room. Then pointed a gun at them.

***

Ryan and Simon sprinted through the trees. Ryan grunted, trying to keep up as the meds did their work. Simon's speed was not something he would have believed if he weren't here to see it himself.

About an hour ago, Ryan had limped out towards Simon's truck, but Simon had marched across his yard to meet him.

"Simon, wait, you don't under -"

Simon had grabbed him by the collar and punched him in the face, then in the gut. Ryan buckled at the waist and fell forward.

Simon pulled him back up. "I practically saved your life!" He shoved Ryan down by the shoulders and kneed him in the chest at the same time. Then flung him sideways. Ryan sprawled on the grass, too weak to fight back. "Did you touch my daughter? Did you?"

"No, I swear!" He shielded his face with his arms as Simon came at him, kicking.

"What about Teagan? Are they both alive?"

"Yes - I mean, no I didn't - Simon, we need to -"

"Don't talk to me! I don't want to hear another word!" He kicked him again, in the stomach this time. The pain and drugs ravaged his insides. He felt searing heat rising from his stomach, then he threw up. Moments later Simon jerked him up by his hood, half dragged him across the yard, and shoved him against the passenger door. "You're having an affair with my wife." Bitterness and quiet rage. Ryan could barely breathe and tried to steady himself under Simon's grasp. He allowed himself to meet Simon's eyes and held his gaze, just like he'd forced himself to do with the girls. It earned him another shot to the face. Then Simon yanked the door open and pushed Ryan inside, slammed the door and went around to the driver's side.

Ryan had taken in heavy breaths, with his face screwed with frustration and anger. "I want to help you."

"Take me to my daughter. Then I'll finish you." Simon slammed the door and went around to the driver's side. A bottle of pills sat on the dash. He read the blue label and took what he needed, then settled in for what would likely be his last trip alive. If Simon didn't kill him, Lydia would. But as much as Ryan loathed Simon he needed him to stay strong to drive, and run through the woods in case the drugs didn't set in quick enough. They had driven in silence.

***

"Lydia?" Annie gasped.

"Thought you held all of daddy's cards, didn't you? That you could live the high life forever with your 'little 'rich girl' status?" She snarled. "Well, all good things come to an end, my dear." She cocked the gun.

"Lydia, please -" A thought struck her "Was it someone in your family who died? Because of dad?" Jada re-entered the room at that moment and innocently bunted Lydia's elbow - the gun fired and sent a bullet into the wall behind them. They screamed and Teagan grabbed Annie's elbow and sprinted forward, shoving Lydia into the doorframe as they pushed past. She shrieked and fired two more shots in their direction. Jada shot ahead barking wildly. They made it to the room beyond their confines and pulled up, spinning for answers. The stairs would make them easy targets.

"Come on!" Teagan yanked them in the direction of the dark tunnel. Annie felt her heart drop as they ran.

When have your crazy ideas ever panned out? She silently screamed at Teagan. *This doesn't feel safe!* Darkness engulfed them and she heard Jada race ahead. Dogs could see in the dark, right? She had no idea if that were true. She groped in the darkness and found cold rock beneath her fingers.

BANG! BANG!

In the next instant, she was on the ground. The cool earth pressed beneath her stomach. Her head rang and the loud shots still echoed off the walls. Had she been shot? Jada's paws scratched the surface nervously. Teagan's hand still grasped her arm.

"Where are you little trouble makers?" A flashlight shone off the rock wall ahead of the them.

They were going to die.

"Daddy's money isn't going to save you this time. And neither is your coach boyfriend! WHERE ARE YOU?" Two more shots fired. They covered their heads and stifled their screams. Suddenly a low hissing came from somewhere nearby. Annie looked around frantically. The light from Lydia's flashlight hit the floor beside her and she quickly rolled back against Teagan. It continued to move towards the sound and suddenly illuminated wooden crates. The light hovered curiously. There were three large letters on each box: TN –

"Dynamite!" Teagan screamed and jumped up, dragging Annie with her back toward the entrance. Back toward the extended gun. But there was no time to think.

"What?" Lydia shrieked, as they whipped past. She tore behind them and the three women broke back into the light of the bunker. Teagan reached the stairs first, but Lydia yanked her backward and shoved her to the floor, then went up first. Jada was on her heels. Annie's heart pounded as she stumbled to pull Teagan up the stairs with her.

***

The two men bolted through the trees. Ryan lagged behind now. Lydia's Lexus had sat at the edge of the forest, off the main road when they pulled up. She couldn't have gotten there too much ahead of them, but there was no way to tell for sure. Simon still refused to believe she was violent.

Ryan's legs weren't following his mind and he stumbled, wasting precious -

BOOM!

The ground shook and he fell to his knees. Not fifty meters away a wall of fierce orange and black smoke exploded skyward.

"No!" Ryan's curdled yell came up against the dark smoke. Simon's eyes went wide and he held his hands out to stop running, mouth gaping. Ryan scrambled to his feet and tried to run, but his disoriented body propelled downward and he fell. Simon ran past him into the embers. Ryan tried again to follow, but collapsed again. He hollered and smashed the ground with his fist.

J. M. Bergman

Chapter 18

Simon choked as he tried to breathe through the mask of smoke and tears on his face. Orange flames burned around dying trunks and black smoke swirled around like a heavy fog as they ran. "Annie! An -" He coughed, tried to take a breath, and coughed again, spitting to the side. He cupped his hands around his mouth. "Teagan!" He couldn't see more than three feet ahead and moved as fast as his lungs allowed.

Smoke billowed around his windbreaker and coated his wet face with thick toxins. He stooped to see below the smoke and pushed forward shielding his eyes. But his eyes ached to keep open so he squeezed them shut, hoping to produce some tears to cool the pain. Without warning his feet began to slide down and the ground disappeared. He propelled his arms wildly trying to regain his balance, but the earth slid out from beneath him. "AH!" He twisted and grasped at empty air.

He saw it then, as a small space cleared in the smoke - the deep, gaping hole about to swallow him. His life would end here today - his career, ambitions, family - what he had left of a family, anyway. His feet lost contact with the ground and he surrendered to the fall. But then two arms grabbed him around his chest and yanked him backward. The body behind him slipped and grunted, but the arms still held him. His rescuer groaned and hollered with one final yank and pulled Simon against his chest. The two men fell backward. The other man softened the fall, but Simon still felt his breath knocked out of him. He could feel his rescuer's chest rising and falling as he lay partially over the man's chest and arm. He was too stunned to move, and instead blinked up at the gray sky, watching orange embers fly upward and burn out. Where had today gone sideways? His daughter was supposed to be released in a civil manner. He and Lydia had planned to make Annie's favorite meal and had bought her a puppy as a welcome home gift. But now he was in a burning forest and loss was beginning to set into his heart.

He rolled onto his hands and knees and stared at the ground, the only stable thing within reach. He focused on being present in this moment.

God, where are you?

He tried to look back up at the sky, but his dry throat was so dry he started coughing again. He shook his head.

You said you save those who love you - haven't I told you that I love you? I trusted you to bring Annie home…

255

He felt a tear slip down his cheek.

"I will protect you."

Simon looked up again. Where had that voice come from? He looked to his side and saw Ryan, still laying on his back, breathing rapidly and coughing. His pants were torn around the knees and his clothes and skin were covered in ash.

Ryan had saved his life.

Simon inched forward and looked ahead to peer into the hole: an enormous black crater loomed below. But why would Ryan save him? What could he possibly gain by helping him?

"My plans are bigger than your plans."

Is that you, God? I don't understand. Simon gazed around again, then back over his shoulder to see if someone had followed them. No one else was there.

Don't give up. It' won't be easy, but I won't leave you.

This time the voice wasn't audible, but it was still separate from his own thoughts somehow. Simon shook his head again and tried to clear his thoughts. Was all this smoke making him hallucinate? Probably. He took a shaky breath and looked sideways again to where Ryan had propped himself up and was watching him. They locked eyes, but Simon didn't have words. He opened his mouth to speak, but realized how foolish he'd sound and stopped. *'Sorry for the beating...thanks for saving me...'* After a moment Ryan nodded once. Simon took a breath and nodded back. They sat listening to the trees burn for a moment.

256

"Lydia!" Simon's guttural scream filled the air. A tree fell nearby. "Annie!" The salty tears on his face pushed over his smoke-stained skin. Lydia couldn't be part of this. They'd kissed before work. Just this morning. Ryan was a liar. A con-artist. For all Simon knew, Ryan may have brought him out here to frame him for Annie's death. He began to shake with sobs. He'd never felt more alone in his life. Where was his beautiful wife? Was that actually *her* Lexus he'd seen at the edge of the forest? How had he been so foolish to believe she was out here in this mess? Sure, he'd gotten no response on her cell, but it wouldn't be the first time she was preoccupied. She was probably back in the city at some fancy coffee shop, laughing with her friends. Enjoying the immaculate lifestyle he'd provided, and looking forward to seeing him after his day at work.

Another tree collapsed, sending ash particles free to fly around their faces. He followed their ascent; particles going to higher places with no purpose. Like his life. He choked again. Now that Ryan Grey had him right where he'd wanted all along, he'd never see his wife or daughter again. The daughter whom he hardly knew anymore. He couldn't even remember what she'd been wearing the last time he saw her. Ryan had probably killed her already and was planning how to kill him next. Then he'd run away with Lydia.

So why did he save me?

It didn't matter. A flame started through his windbreaker but he didn't care. Why struggle? There was nothing left to live for at this point. His patients would find a new doctor and life would go on without him.

"Simon Jeffreys, don't give up!"

That voice. The hallucinating voice that knew his name. That's all it was. He shook his head again and stared straight ahead. He would die right here without a fight. No need for Ryan to do anything hostile to him.

Suddenly a flash of white caught his attention and vanished back into the smoke. He swallowed and strained to see it again. Ryan jolted upright beside him; he'd seen it too. Perhaps they were both hallucinating… They waited. Blistering sounds of the burning forest surrounded them. There it was again! White against the smoke, but then it disappeared. Simon sat up straight and searched for substance in the mess around him. Smoke burned into his eyelids, but he refused to blink. All at once a large Husky leapt out of the smoke and charged for them, bounding over the charred ground and dodging falling debris. Ryan leapt to his feet just as the dog crashed into his embrace and flattened him. The excited beast jumped uncontrollably over his body.

***

Ryan let Jada jump over his body and nearly dig a hole into his sides with her snout. She whined and barked and slobbered his face. He wrapped his arms around her frantic body and spoke softly to her. "Good girl. It's okay, Jada. I'm here. It's okay." He kissed her head and continued to reassure her. Eventually she slowed down and let him hold her. She was covered with ash, but her eyes were clear and it didn't look like any bones were broken. She'd escaped from the bunker. How did she get out and who escaped with her? He held her nervous head and looked steadily into her scared eyes. "Jada, it's okay. I'm here now. You're okay." He pressed his head against hers and noticed Simon watching them.

"Was your dog with my daughter?" His defeated eyes held a drop of hope. Ryan kissed Jada again, then got to his feet and offered Simon a hand. Simon hesitated, but then accepted it and stood

"Yes, Jada was with them. I don't know how she would have gotten out without help."

"Gotten out of what?" Simon stared at him with the longing Ryan imagined all parents felt when they had hope that they could see their lost child again. But the images from this morning of the girl's nearly frozen bodies came to his memory then, and he didn't want to tell Simon any more than he needed to know.

"The explosion, this big hole - it was an underground bunker."

Simon's jaw dropped and he grabbed Ryan's sweater with both hands, pulling him within inches of his face. "You had my daughter underground?" He hissed. Darkness swept across his face. "You -" He breathed the word through a snarl and took another threatening step forward. "What did you do to her?"

"I swear, nothing sexual happened." He held his palms up. "I swear. Simon there's so much to explain - but Jada made it out, which means Annie might have made it out too. We have to keep looking. I know you don't believe me, but Lydia came here to kill her." He licked his lips and watched Simon's expression changing. "I'll explain everything after we find her. I promise." Simon stared at him a moment, then shoved his fists against Ryan's chest and let go. Ryan narrowed his eyes, but didn't waste time getting upset. He knelt back down. "Jada, where are they?" He held her head gingerly again. "Where are Annie and Teagan." She barked and whipped her head away, then ran ahead of them back around the crater. "Come on!" Ryan shouted back to Simon. He couldn't be sure that Jada understood him but all he could do was follow her and hope for the best. He made his way around the crater as quickly as he could, side stepping around fallen branches and watching his feet so he didn't trip. He took a quick backward glance to make sure Simon was still there, but stumbled and face-planted. Everything went black and he couldn't breathe. But a second later he was being pulled up, and heat and light flashed in front of him. He staggered and fell back to his knees.

"I'm not leaving you here." He was being pulled up again. "Ryan! Get up!" He tried to balance and reached back for the hands holding him up.

"Okay, okay, I'm fine." He stumbled again, but pushed himself back up this time and took a couple steps. He glanced back and saw Simon just before the anxious man ran into him.

"Let's go, Ryan!"

He scoffed and turned to run again. Jada had disappeared. He ran both hands through his hair, then decided to run straight. He'd taken a handful of steps when the ground sloped downwards. *Another crater?* He flailed, but lost his footing and began to slide. "Simon, stop!" He tried to yell back, and swore as he thrashed his arms for something to grab to stop the fall. His fist closed around a thin branch of leaves which slid through his hand as he continued to slide down, fast. Then his feet hit the ground and he fell forward to his knees. Simon grunted behind him, then tumbled and landed on him, sending Ryan sprawling. Ryan rolled over and shoved Simon off. Just ahead of them, a line of trees stood beyond the thinning smoke. They ran through it together, and Ryan stopped short. Simon collided with him again and nearly knocked him over.

"Take one more step and I'll blow their brains out!" Lydia screamed. She stood directly behind Annie with her gun pointed at Annie's head. Her blonde hair was singed and filthy, and her clothes were covered in ash. "I'm not messing around, Simon! I will kill your pathetic attempt at a daughter if you come any closer!"

"Lydia!" Simon stepped forward and she fired at the sky, just as Ryan blocked him with his arm. Annie gasped at the sound and squeezed her eyes shut, sending tears down her face. Her large sweater was burnt in places and hung from her raised arms, and her lips were quivering. Teagan stood next to her, jeans seared and blackened as if she'd been dragged over the ashy, forest floor. Her hands were trembling, but her eyes were filled with anger instead of fear. "Lydia, what do you want?" Simon tried to push past, but Ryan stepped in front of him and blocked him again.

"Listen to your little sidekick, Simon! I'm prepared to shoot all four of you!"

***

"Dad…" Annie cried through small breaths. It hardly made sense that they were still alive after just barely escaping the explosion. Lydia pushed the lid open and got through with Jada first. Annie tried to follow but Lydia had let the lid fall shut over them. It had been heavy, but she managed to push it open again and reach back for Teagan.

"Go!" Teagan had screamed, climbing up and tripping as Annie pulled her arm. The explosion had gone off less than ten seconds after they got out and began to run. Annie had felt her body shoot forward from the shock wave with a wall of heat at her back. She'd landed on her knees and tumbled down the slope. The dying bushes cut her hands and face on the way down. Not many people could survive to share an escape story like that. And now it looked like they'd made it out just to get shot in the head in front of her dad.

Her father tried to push past Ryan again. "Annie, I've missed you so much." His voice cracked. So close to being rescued, but still only a step away from death. "Lydia. what's going on? I'll give you anything you want." His voice cracked again.

"Can you bring back the dead?" She spat.

He lifted his hands in front of him. "What are you talking about?"

"Beverley Clere. You killed her, Simon!" She coughed to the side. Her dad looked at the ground, searching for meaning. Annie longed to answer all his questions and take the sadness away from his face. Ryan lowered his arm.

"Trial AB100: She was my patient..." Simon pulled at his goatee. "That was so long ago, Lydia - how do you know about that? I don't understand."

"She was Alec's wife. His pregnant wife!"

He held his hands open with a blank expression. "Beverley was Alec's wife?"

"See? You don't even remember her! You *used* her for your drug experiments!" She cocked the weapon. "I don't know how you sleep at night!"

"I hardly sleep at night. Lydia! And maybe if you were home more often, instead of spending the night with other men, you'd know that!"

"How dare you accuse me of being unfaithful!" She shrieked.

"He's right here, Lydia!" Simon's face was turning red. "I'm done with your little games and lies! If you weren't happy you should have just told me - I would have given you anything you wanted in a divorce. And what does any of this have to do with Annie and Teagan?"

"Her life for theirs, Simon! And you murdered my nephew!"

"So, you think killing these innocent girls will make us even?" Her dad's body was shaking and he took a step forward. Annie bit her lip in surprise at his tone and the fact that he was actually arguing. He'd never risen his voice or disagreed with Lydia in their home.

"Oh, no, this is part two, Simon. You still think it was an accident that your wife died in a car accident? Alec made sure his truck hit her taxi hard." She sneered. Annie's eyes filled with tears as her dad stumbled backward. His face turned pale with a look of horror and he fell sideways, barely catching himself on a tree trunk. He started taking deep breaths and fell to the ground, one knee at a time. Saliva began to drizzle out of his mouth. "You took his wife and child, Simon! This is justice!" No one spoke for a minute.

Simon spit and wiped his mouth on his sleeve. "You never thought to bring this up at home? Where we could talk like civilized humans?" His face had skewed with anger and sadness." He spit again. "All these years we've been together, you've been what? Alec's pawn? Waiting for the perfect time to strike and kill us? Beverly was part of a medical trial, Lydia! She signed for it. She knew the risks!"

"Risks? And yet you assured her and Alec your science experiment would work!"

"It was a trial!"

Annie couldn't watch anymore and looked at Ryan and was surprised again that he was staring at her. His eyes shot to the side and back. She crinkled her eyebrows in question. One of his arms hung just behind his leg. He moved his eyes again. She understood and dipped her chin slightly.

"- is what you deserve!" Lydia shouted.

"I could have helped Alec! Why would you keep this from me all these years?" Tears began to stream down his face. "Lydia, please…let's talk about this...

"It's too late to talk -"

Annie dove sideways to the ground and heard the knife fly from Ryan's hand. It whistled for a second, then plunged into Lydia's chest. Lydia stumbled backwards, mouth gaping. Her dad's jaw dropped with horror. Annie kicked the back of Lydia's leg, hard, causing her to fall awkwardly, then collapse onto her back, gasping for air. She rasped wordless sounds and her hands and legs started to twitch as the knife's handle protruded from her body.

Could this be another nightmare?

Annie closed her eyes for a second, wondering if she'd wake up in the bunker. But no, when she opened her eyes she was laying on grass, between a river and a burning forest. Her dad was on his knees bent over Lydia's body. His mouth opened and closed several times. As if he would vomit any second.

"Lydia... Lydia... no, no…" He held her head and stroked her hair.

Annie forced herself to look away. She felt dizzy and nauseous, and grasped at the ground to make sure she wasn't moving. Her fingers pressed into the cool surface and she focused on pushing herself away, as far as she could go. Away from death and tears and brokenness. Teagan was still standing and now lowered her hands from her head to take in what had just happened. She gaped at Lydia's twitching body, looked incredulously at Annie, then back to Lydia, and back. Annie looked away and saw Ryan. Their eyes met and he immediately looked away, but not before his mouth twisted and his face began to break with emotion. He grabbed the back of his neck with both hands.

J. M. Bergman

Chapter 19

Lydia was dying. Another minute or so and she would be gone. At his hands. Ryan stared up the embankment and choked back on his tears. She'd used him, and yet their relationship had felt real. And he had loved her, even after she berated him in his home and here in front of everyone. If there had been a way to save her from her own dark heart he would have done everything he could to help her. But she'd been brainwashed by Alec for too long.

And she was Simon's wife.

Ryan realized then what an idiot he'd been for allowing himself to be led away by Lydia's reasoning - Simon was a good man and a good father. What he'd done as a doctor didn't even come close in comparison with what Ryan had done as a teen. And now after everyone's lives were messed up, Ryan would still lose everything he'd worked for. His team, his clients, people's respect. Everyone would know who he really was. Ryan Grey: *the murderer.* The man who witnessed little boys trying to adjust in a hostage environment and failed to save every single one of them. The man who murdered his parents, kidnapped and tortured teenage girls, stole a million of dollars and helped rip a family apart. And now he'd killed his lover. He closed his eyes and let the accusations paint themselves over his body. Then he heard Lydia's sputtered dying words to Simon and turned back.

"Never - loved - you." Blood spewed through her teeth. Simon's chest was heaving with emotion and his face was twisted with his sobs. Lydia coughed up more blood and Simon lifted her shoulders to help. "Just let me die!"

"Lydia - no, no!" Simon choked, shaking his head. He stared at her dying face. Ryan swallowed and caught Teagan watching him. He turned and clenched his teeth together. After everything he'd done, Lydia had nothing to say to him. She'd played him like a forgotten toy. And he'd allowed it.

"Al -" She coughed and managed a deep, gurgling scream. Ryan spun, and his heart pulled desperately toward her. He wanted to hold her. To take the pain away. She spat and grinned. "Al - Al - Alec will - " She gasped savagely, hyperventilating and choking at the same time. Life and light left her wide open eyes. Simon coughed on a sob and grabbed her hand. His body began to shake as he wept.

Tears streamed down Annie's quiet face. Teagan gaped, then moved away from the body, toward another place on the slope. Ryan swallowed again and wiped his tears with the bottoms of his palms. And then panic rose like fire in his chest.

Alec. He knew where they were. And he was on his way.

He traced his mouth with his fingers. They wouldn't have much time. As if on cue, the sound of a small engine came from across a nearby brook; perhaps a four-wheeler. Carrying the man who had orchestrated this whole scheme. He'd kill all four of them.

"We have to go", Ryan said, hoping the fear in his thoughts wouldn't echo in his words. Annie was the only one to acknowledge him. "Hey! This isn't over. Alec is coming!" He pointed in the direction the sound came from. "He'll kill us!"

Simon lifted his head. Ash and dirt mixed with remorse on his face. "Alec?"

"Dad, we should go." Annie scrambled to her feet. She glanced between Ryan and Simon as if deciding which man was in charge. The approaching engine grew closer. Probably no more than four hundred meters away.

"Mr. Jeffreys, we have to go!" Teagan jogged toward him. Annie joined her and they each took an arm. Simon was scrunching his face and shaking his head.

"No, no, Alec would never -"

"Dad! He planned this! He's going to kill us!"

"No! No, you're wrong! Lydia, wake up, sweetheart. Lydia. Lydia!" Annie pulled at his arm and Teagan did the same. "No! Lydia!" He yanked his arms free and reached for her dead face. Ryan's stomach churned and he dragged his hand over his face. Then he took charge.

"Ladies, get back." He stalked toward them. Annie stared, wide-eyed, but stepped away. He bent down, met Simon's eyes briefly and ripped out his knife. Simon gawked and his neck jerked forward as if he would convulse. Ryan wiped the knife clean against Lydia's jeans. "Simon, it's finished. Your 'missing daughter' is over there." He tilted his head toward her and stood. "Leave now or you're a dead man. But Annie and Teagan are coming with me."

"No!" Simon bolted upright, then collapsed and began to convulse.

"Dad!" Annie cried. She ran to him and dropped to the ground beside him. The four-wheeler sounded just beyond their sight. They'd have less than a minute to get a head start. Ryan made the decision, grabbed Annie around the waist and started back toward the embankment.

"Ryan, wait! Dad! Dad!" She screamed and tried to pull away, but he threw her over his shoulder as he'd done so many times before.

"Teagan, let's go." He ordered and they started up the slope.

"Dad! Dad!" Annie kicked and squirmed. She pounded Ryan's back with her fists and kicked at his abs. "Ryan! No! We can't leave him here!" Thinning smoke enveloped them as they re-entered the fallout zone, and Jada shot past and ran ahead. He could hear Teagan close behind. Alec could be on their heels right away, depending on how long he spent with Lydia's body. Or if he stayed behind to kill Simon and relish his death. A black tree fell just inches from his face.

He sidestepped and threw an arm back to redirect Teagan in case she hadn't seen it. She hadn't and he shoved her shoulder out of the way.

"- my choice, Ryan! Put me down!" Annie continued to scream. He swung her to the ground and grabbed her shoulders.

"Hey, listen to me! You want to go back there so Alec can shoot you? That means Lydia wins. Do you want that?" He choked on a cloud of smoke and coughed into his sleeve. Ash and timber fell from a nearby tree. Her lips trembled below her glassy eyes.

"But, I can't leave him!" Her voice cracked. Something crossed her face, as if she realized she would never see him again. She looked past Ryan to where they'd just ran from, probably hoping Simon would run through the burning trees. But he didn't and her shoulders fell. Ryan let out a breath and loosened his grip.

"Alright, are you ready to go?" But she leapt out of his grasp and sprinted away. "Hey!" He spun and grasped at the air, but she made a clean break. Teagan sidestepped and grabbed her.

"Annie, please, you can't go back there!"

"Let go, Teagan!" She broke away and stumbled backward, then turned to run back. Ryan pushed past Teagan and grabbed Annie by the shoulder.

"You're coming with us, now!" He barked.

"Run, Annie!" Surprised, they both turned to see Simon running toward them. Annie listened and ran. *Finally*. Ryan tore ahead of the group to lead the way. Smoke burned his lungs as he ran past burning skeletons of the forest he loved. Another smoldering tree fell across his path. He managed to stop in time and jump over. The billowing, dark smoke had turned from black to gray. With any luck, Alec would get lost in this mess, or go down in the crater. Ryan slowed his pace. The dark hole would come up soon, and he strained to see the ground ahead. Smoke continued to rise from the parched, blackened dirt. He slowed to a walk and extended his hand backward to signal them to slow down. He glanced over his shoulder to make sure the group understood. Teagan nodded and Annie pulled up behind her. Simon had fallen behind, but they didn't have time to stop. He'd have to find his own way.

"Hold hands, you two." He ordered. It came across as a childish command, but he didn't trust Annie to stay with them, and he doubted either of them were thinking clearly. He squinted ahead. Jada had disappeared too. He ripped off a dead branch and used it to secure walking space ahead of them. About a minute later they came upon the crater. He breathed a sigh of relief to know he'd found it. Once around they'd be clear to run. And if all went well, it would swallow Alec. He glanced back and saw both girls holding each other, waiting for his leadership.

***

Simon stumbled and fell. He wiped his eyes and strained to see Annie's heels running ahead. But she had disappeared. He coughed and covered his nose and mouth with his windbreaker. He heard a crack above and he saw a flaming branch fall just in time to dodge it.

So many questions pounded his exhausted heart. Could his entire marriage really have been built on vengeance? There must have been signs…but he'd missed them. Even missed the signs of her affair. But he'd never once considered Ryan as his love opponent. The young man was hardly more than a youth. The fact that Lydia stooped to such a relationship for this horrendous cause showed how sick and twisted her mind was. He glanced back. Still no sign of Alec, his brother-in-law. The one he'd shared holidays with. Fishing trips and camping season. Christmas dinners. This man visited in his home and, sadly, it was true - Simon had forgotten about him as the grieving husband of Beverly Clere.

And now Ryan Grey had his daughter again. Literally had ripped her out of his grasp. The criminal had managed to singlehandedly take away the two most important people in his life in a matter of minutes. And with every step he ran, he hated Ryan more. Alec would find him eventually. And then what? They'd have a chat about Lydia's unfortunate involvement and death? No. One of them would die. If he surrendered to Alec's will, maybe it would be enough to end this ongoing nightmare. And maybe his dear daughter would be left alone...with Ryan Grey. Simon closed his eyes for a moment. Orphaning her after everything she'd gone through because of his mistakes would be unbearable. Surrendering wasn't an option. He took another look around. And ran. He had to survive for her.

Even though he hated Ryan, the truth was that Ryan was smart about finding his way around in this forest. He'd brought him to Annie's rescue with seconds to spare and saved him from falling to his death. Annie's expression when she begged him to leave with Ryan said a thousand words too - she trusted him. Simon looked back once more and detoured to the side. Now he was jogging away from where he believed they had run. Annie's part in his mistakes was over. No use Alec finding all four of them together. Alec's real battle was with him. Simon ripped a piece of his burnt windbreaker off with his teeth and dropped it behind for Alec to follow.

When Alec found him, there would be war. Lydia's death and Annie's abduction were on Alec's head.

***

"Keep moving!" Ryan shouted back. Teagan pulled up and bent at the waist breathing hard. Annie had broken free from Teagan and stood staring back into the smoky trees. "Annie, let's go!" Her tangled hair was mixed with ash and dirt and hung down her back. She glanced at them and took a step back the way they had come. Ryan grunted and pulled at the nape of his neck to try and control his irritation. He was a changed man now, he reminded himself, and anger and muscle needed to be secondary to his thinking. But patience didn't grow in an instant. He ran back to her and she turned.

"Kid, you want to die today, or what -"

She shoved him in the chest and almost pushed him back a step. "Stop talking to me like that! My step-mom and Uncle are killers, and my dad might die! He's alone and probably so confused." She gazed back. "What if -"

"If Alec caught up with him?" Ryan grabbed her wrists and stopped her from moving. "Then your dad will deal with it like an adult. There's nothing else you can do."

She twisted her lips and looked back to the trees. "But, he's alone! What if -"

"If he got hurt? He's a doctor, Annie, he'll figure it out! Do you think he'd want you to risk your life going back for him?"

"No, but -"

"No, he wouldn't! Do you get it?"

"Hey! Back off, Ryan!" Teagan shoved between them. Ryan looked ready to burst into one of his angry fits, but she ignored him and wrapped Annie into a hug. "Your dad will find his way out." She stroked Annie's back while they both cried. Ryan pinched the bridge of his nose and looked at the trees behind them, almost expecting Alec to emerge from the smoke.

"Okay, are you two done?"

"Ryan!" Teagan whirled back to him. "We just watched you kill Lydia! And Annie's dad was crying all over the place! I've never seen something like what happened back there. You'd probably show more patience with Jada if she were as traumatized as we are!"

"Because she'd be reasonable and get over it!" Even before he'd said it he knew he sounded ridiculous. Teagan dropped her jaw and shook her head, then turned back to where Annie was wiping her eyes.

"Come on, girl. We're almost free. We can do this." She grabbed her hand. Then they both looked up at him.

"Okay, I want you two running in front of me where I can see you." He nodded and they started again. They ran for another fifteen minutes, with Ryan letting shouting directions from behind. Finally, the edge of the woods came into sight, not more than a hundred metres away. Sweat ran down his forehead. This nightmare was almost finished. He'd get the girls to safety in a hotel or something and wait for the cops there. Then turn Alec in. And then the world would know the real Ryan Grey. He closed his eyes and exhaled. No more running. Time to man up and take responsibility for what he'd done so many years ago, and the pain he'd caused these two and their families. He pulled up and rested his fists at his side. These were his last moments of freedom. He looked around at his dead, beloved forest. It was time to leave this behind. Regardless of what the future held.

The girls stopped just before the treeline and glanced back at him. He motioned them forward with his hand. They hadn't tried to escape from him here in the woods, and perhaps that meant that what he'd thought back in the bunker was true. They'd forgiven him and somehow saw him beyond his crimes.

Is that how God sees me too?

He'd have to ask Annie later. If he got the chance before they locked him up. He shook away the negative thought.

Where was Jada? He whistled, turned, and whistled again. Then waited. No sign of her. He looked back towards the woods and contemplated going back. No, not yet. He'd make sure the girls were okay and safely out of the burning forest. She was a smart dog. She'd find her way to the road. One last breath and he jogged for the treeline. He broke through into the sunlight and immediately shielded his eyes with his hand.

"Hey there, pretty boy."

Ryan's stomach dropped and he nearly started to throw up. He turned slowly. "What —"

"You didn't tell me you had two lovely, little girlfriends stashed away out here." Wade had one arm around both girls, at gunpoint. "Before we get any further: drop the knife. I know you've got it."

Ryan tried to catch his breath and make sense of this. "How -?" He bent at the waist and pressed his hands on his hips. "What are you doing here?"

"I said, 'drop it'. Then we'll talk." Ryan gawked and turned over every possibility of getting around this. But he couldn't do any of them. Not with the girls being held at gunpoint. He surrendered one hand to his side and pulled the knife case out of his back pocket. He held both hands open and dropped it. "Did everybody see that? We can get along. Just do as I say and nobody gets hurt." Wade grinned down at the top of the girl's heads. Familiar heat spread up Ryan's spine.

"Ryan...?" Teagan squeaked.

Wade gently shook her shoulder. "Shhh, don't worry, my girl. Pretty boy, I don't know what kind of trouble you got into with that well-to-do looking gentleman back in town, or why he gave you that beating - but I'm sure you enjoyed that more than what I had planned for you." He winked. "He pulled up at your place right before I did. I thought I'd let him go at you first. But now it's my turn."

Annie's eyes widened as she put the pieces together, but she didn't say anything. Ryan took a breath.

"Okay." He nodded once, trying to look brave. "I'll do whatever you want. Leave them alone."

Wade laughed. "And give up the chance for an even bigger party? Not on your life." Two sets of glittering, young eyes stared at Ryan for answers, but he was speechless. And unarmed. He tried to think of something to say - anything that would calm their nerves. But his mouth opened and closed without speaking. Because anything he said would be a lie. Wade's amused expression turned serious. "However, I don't need them both, so I'm only going to ask you once -" He cocked his gun. "Get into my truck."

Ryan swallowed and lifted both hands, and placed them on his head. He started to walk across the highway to where Wade's truck was waiting, but stopped to look the girls in the eyes. "Do whatever he tells you to." Then he closed the distance to the truck. One more glance back at the girls, then he took a breath and pulled himself up into the cab. The interior smelled of dark wood and warm spice, mixed with sweet tobacco. Wade's scent. Ryan kept his hands visible and held Annie and Teagan's trembling eyes with a steady expression.

"There. See, we're getting better at this." Wade grinned again, then pushed the girls ahead of him. "Hop in, you two. We're going on a little trip."

Continued in:

'The Phoenix Scar'

Excerpt

The Phoenix Scar

Teagan wiped her bound hands across her face. Heavy footsteps crunched through the forest behind her. The violence she'd witnessed today had been awful. Even too terrible to wish on someone like Lydia. But she knew better than to jump in the middle and try to be a hero – unlike Annie. What on earth had snapped in Annie's mind to make her throw herself into a fight that had nothing to do with her. It was only luck that she hadn't been hit or seriously injured. Teagan shook her head, trying to clear the images again, as she'd done all evening. Her foot halted abruptly and she fell forward, flailing for substance and trying to rebalance, but her foot was still caught.

Thump! She hit the dark ground, which was closer than what she thought. Her mouth filled with dirt and blood.

"Ouch. Sweetheart, are you alright?" Wade's arms came from behind and wrapped around her shoulders, as he helped her to her knees. Had she blacked out a second? She couldn't remember, in fact, she could hardly feel the pain in her face, and yet, her whole body felt jarred. She licked at the blood on her lips, then wiped it on her sleeve.

"Yeah, I'm fine." She brushed away dirt and debris from her chest.

"Just relax. Let's take a seat and breathe for a minute." He was hunched in front of her and his white smile shone in the dark woods. A cool autumn breeze snuck past. "Tell me something about yourself, Freckles. I don't know much you."

She licked her lips again, knowing she didn't want to tell him anything, but scared of what he'd do to her if she didn't answer. "I'm not afraid of snakes."

"Ha! That's right. Unfortunately, you got to see that I am. What else?"

Her face felt colder than before. It'd be better to keep moving. "I don't know. Um… I like sports."

"Okay, so you're one of Ryan's soccer girls, aren't you? He treats you good?"

'Don't mention the scars.' Ryan's command. She looked at the ground.

"Yeah. He does."

"Hmm, okay, that's good. How you feeling? Ready to keep walking?" He helped her up and they continued through the trees for another fifteen minutes. "I'm going to climb up to the highway and make a phone call, assuming I find service up there. I need you to stay here, okay?"

"Why can't I come with you?" The forest felt darker at the thought of being left alone in the eerie shadows.

"This is a private phone call, Missy. Can I trust you, or should I tie you to one of these trees?" That escalated fast. She waited for him to crack a joke and slap her on the shoulder. But he just stared at her silently.

"You don't need to do that. I'll stay here."

"Okay, because if I turn around and see that you've followed me, our friendship will take a little dip. Do you understand?" Was he threatening her? No, he couldn't be, because he'd used the term 'friendship'. That meant they had a connection now. "You won't like it", he said, as if he knew what she was thinking. So, it was a threat.

"I understand." But she didn't.

"There's my girl." He slapped her shoulder then. "Alright, just relax here until I get back. I won't be long. And if you're good, I'll cut your hands free for the walk back." He turned and disappeared around the trees ahead. She felt as if the forest' shadows were closing in around her. His footsteps crunched over the ground as he got further away. She listened carefully to the silence that came after.

And then followed him.

She was light on her feet and had often been told she walked like a ghost. She moved slowly on her toes, and the forest floor barely stirred beneath her. She could hear his faint voice about twenty metres up the slope, beyond the treeline. Sounds of the quiet stream, calmly pouring over the earth, played in the background. She inched right to the edge of the tree's covering. The moonlight shone off his silhouette.

"- small delay. Two days, tops -" He paused. "Vehicle trouble. I know – you don't need to tell me how important time is!" He checked over his shoulder, probably to see if she were listening. She knew she was covered by shadows, but still didn't dare to move. "He's with me, and I've got two fresh souls you're gonna love. Girls." He started down the highway, towards the bridge, and his voice travelled away with him. She bit her broken lip and contemplated. Why couldn't she know the contents of this conversation? This was information about their fate, which she wanted to be prepared for. It was her life and she deserved to know! Just as she built up the nerve to sneak along the trees, he turned and started walking back. "- an estimate. We'll stay at Eagle Eye Pass tomorrow." He lowered his hand from his ear, and she darted back into the trees.

She should have started back sooner because her quick feet were more difficult to keep quiet than her soft, intentional steps had been. Each movement sounded magnified. *Crunch! Crunch! Whoosh!* One foot fell into a hole of sorts. She gasped and landed on her knees, then scrambled back up to her feet.

Crunch! Crunch! He was coming!

She ran as fast as she could. *Smack!* A branch of pines hit her face. She stumbled backward, but forced herself to keep moving. No point in trying to hide now. Maybe she could beat him back to the camp site and make something up. She held her hands out like a shield and ducked against flying branches.

Crunch! Crunch! Crunch! Crunch! The heavy steps were running close behind her now. He was coming for her!